MOUNTAIN ROMANCE

Still haunted by the tragic death of her young husband seven years earlier, Beth Tennant has worked to build the life he'd have wanted for herself and their young son Luke. But her business, a guest house in a stunning corner of the Lake District, is running short of cash; and to make matters worse, her estranged brother-in-law unexpectedly turns up. Then when a guest is poisoned, and Luke's safety is threatened, the long-concealed secrets harboured by those Beth trusts most are forced into the open . . .

PAULA WILLIAMS

MOUNTAIN ROMANCE

Complete and Unabridged

LINFORD
Leicester

First published in Great Britain in 2016

First Linford Edition
published 2017

A catalogue record for this book is available
from the British Library.

ISBN 978–1–4448–3331–7

Published by
F. A. Thorpe (Publishing)
Anstey, Leicestershire

Set by Words & Graphics Ltd.
Anstey, Leicestershire
Printed and bound in Great Britain by
T. J. International Ltd., Padstow, Cornwall

This book is printed on acid-free paper

1

Lake District. Seven years earlier.

If only. Someone said that's the saddest phrase in the English language. And they weren't wrong.

If only it had been pouring with rain that morning. Or the mountains had been blotted out by one of those all-too-common November fogs. Or obliterated altogether by a raging blizzard as it careered its way down through the valley.

But as I looked out of the sitting room window and down across the valley, there was no rain, fog or blizzard. It was, in fact, one of those glorious early winter days when the sky was so blue it made your eyes ache to look at it. When the sun sparkled off the tumbling waters of the beck and painted the bracken cloak fell-side in colours of burnt caramel and butterscotch.

It was, I decided, a perfect day to get on with painting the sitting room. I needed to be doing something, anything, rather than going over and over the details of last night's stupid row in my mind. So I got busy, and had already covered the furniture in dust sheets and got out the paint pots when Andrew wandered down.

'I wondered how much longer you were going to be, lazybones.' My laugh was a bit forced as I tried to pretend that everything was normal. 'Come on. Let's crack on then. With a bit of luck we'll get the first coat on by lunchtime.'

I picked up a brush and was about to hand it to him when, for the first time, I noticed what he was wearing. Not the scruffy old jeans and jumper he kept for decorating, but his climbing gear. Even down to his boots and helmet.

I stared at him. 'What are you doing? We agreed, remember? Last weekend we said we'd get this finished today. I thought we could crack on with the decorating this morning, then go and have a pub lunch somewhere.'

He shrugged and turned to the window. 'Yeah, I know, but you can't stay cooped up indoors on an amazing day like this. Look, can't you see? There's snow on the pikes. The first of the year. It'll be brilliant up there.'

'You're going climbing?' In my struggle to stop myself yelling at him, my voice went very quiet. 'Is this about last night?'

'Of course not. This is about it being perfect climbing weather. Nothing more, nothing less.' He pulled me closer to him and kissed the top of my head. 'Why don't you come with us? The painting will still be there tomorrow. The snow might not be. Or, if it is, the weather could close in and make climbing impossible.'

'Us? Who are you going with?'

'Joe, of course.' With his arms still wrapped around me, he checked his watch. 'And I said I'd meet him down by the car park. You know how he goes on about being late.'

'Joe,' I hissed as I pulled myself away, making no attempt to hide the fury that suddenly flared inside me. 'I might have known he'd have something to do with this. Honestly, Andrew, all that precious brother of yours has to do is snap his fingers and you come running.'

'No I don't,' he said, his anger, as always, rising to match mine. That's the way we were — both quick to an anger that burnt fiercely, but usually was swift to end in sweet reconciliation. But not that day. If only . . .

'Not much,' I snapped, unable to let it go.

'What is it with you?' he said. 'I'd have thought, after all he's done for us, you'd be a bit nicer to him. After all, you're always saying we'd never have been able to buy this place if it hadn't been for him.'

'Something that you obviously regret,' I retorted. 'You made that pretty damn clear last night.'

He didn't deny it, but merely shrugged, his gaze drifting towards the window as if he couldn't wait to be out there. 'There's no point arguing with you when you're in this mood,' he muttered.

'Oh, come on, Andrew. Your brother's never made any secret of the fact that he doesn't like me and thinks you should never have married me.'

'Now you're just being ridiculous,' he said. 'It's just he thought we were too young to take on the responsibility of a house. This house in particular.'

'A money pit of a place — that's what he calls Brackwith, isn't it? He thinks that I pushed you into it; that we were both too stupid and naive to see everything that was wrong with it.'

Andrew turned from the window and came towards me, his voice honeyed and cajoling. 'Beth, I haven't got time for this now. Look, sweetheart, we'll talk about it later, OK?'

I shrugged but said nothing.

'And you've got Joe all wrong, you know,' he went on as the silence stretched between us, as taut as a violin string. 'He really does like you. Believe me, if he didn't, you'd know it. It's just . . . well, he's always been a bit overprotective as far as I'm concerned.' He pushed his hand through his hair and gave that little-boy grin that usually melted my heart.

Usually. But not that day. Why oh why didn't I take that one small step towards him that would have put an end to the stupid bickering? He was going to go, I'd known that from the moment I saw him with his climbing gear. So why didn't I just smile and say something jokey about Big Brother?

But I didn't. My heart, far from melting, was as hard and cold as granite. And just as unmoving.

'Since Mum ran out on us and Dad thought he'd find the answer to life's problems at the bottom of a bottle, Joe's taken it on himself to look out for me,' Andrew went on. 'It's just that he can't quite get his head around the idea that I'm twenty-three years old. A grown-up.'

'Then it's a pity you don't start acting like one.' I prised the lid off the tin and began furiously stirring the primrose-yellow paint. 'I was right, wasn't I? This is about last night. That's why you're running off, instead of staying here and talking about it like two sensible adults.'

'I thought we'd done all the talking,' he muttered. 'At least, you did.'

'Then talk to me,' I begged him, ignoring the mulish expression on his face. 'Tell me what you think. How you feel about — '

'No, Beth,' he cut in. 'I don't know what I think, to be honest. Not yet. I'm sorry for what I said last night, as I've already told you a hundred times. It was just such a shock. But for now, I need to get my head round it. And there's no better place for thinking than up on the pikes.'

'You need to think?' The brush slipped from my hand and splashed primrose paint on the floor, adding to my fury and tipping me over the edge;

7

making me say stupid things I didn't really mean. 'What you really mean is you need to talk it through with Joe, don't you? For pity's sake, Andrew, can't we do anything without your brother sticking his oar in — interfering in our lives, the way he always does? I'm absolutely sick of it.'

'He doesn't — '

'Just go, before one of us says or does something we'll regret. Go on. Go.' I picked up a cloth and began rubbing furiously at the spilt paint.

He stood watching me for a second. 'Beth, please — don't be like that.'

'I'll see you later,' I said coldly as I picked up the brush again. 'Now, if you'll excuse me, one of us has to act the grown-up this morning.'

He leant across to kiss me, but — ever the grown-up, that's me — I turned my head, stepped away quickly and began slapping the paint on the wall, not stopping until I heard him give a heavy sigh, followed by a smothered curse as he turned and walked away.

★ ★ ★

Normally I love decorating. There was something soothing and almost hypnotic about the rhythmic swish of the brush across the rough walls that, coupled with the satisfaction of seeing the sludgy green walls beginning to look as fresh and primrose-y as it said on the tin, lifted my mood and made me regret my outburst.

Andrew, I realised, wasn't the only one behaving like a child. I'd more than matched him.

He'd only been gone half an hour when I phoned him, hoping to catch him before he was out of range. But mobile phone signals are conspicuous by their absence in many parts of the Lakeland fells, and the best I could do was leave a voice message.

'Andrew, I'm sorry. I was being a complete moody mare. But then again, you were being a selfish git.' I forced a laugh, to let him know I was joking. 'But you're quite right — the painting

9

would have kept till tomorrow. Take care and I'll see you soon. Love you. Bye.'

Trouble was, there was no tomorrow. At least, not for Andrew.

At twenty past five, I was dicing lamb for his favourite curry (the only thing I was any good at cooking) when there was a knock at the door. A somber-faced policeman with kind eyes stood there.

'Does an Andrew Tennant live here?' he asked.

I nodded, unable to speak as my throat closed over.

'And are you Mrs Tennant?'

I nodded again. But inside my head I was screaming, *No. No. Noooooooo.*

'I'm afraid I have some bad news,' he said quietly. 'May I come in?'

2

If only. Two bloody useless words. There was no point in going over it. But sometimes it was hard not to.

Joe remembered that day like it was yesterday, every detail etched in his brain. Except, of course, for those last few hours that would, according to the medics, probably remain a blank forever. It was a beautiful day, brilliant climbing weather. It started out as one of those glorious days when you feel glad to be alive. It ended . . . Well, I've been able to piece together where it went wrong, at least, from what I've been told. It went something like this.

Joe saw Andrew's beat-up old Mini screech into the car park, spraying a shower of gravel as it did so. He slammed the car door so hard, the noise sent a crowd of rooks in the nearby larch trees spiralling upwards in raucous alarm.

'You OK?' Joe asked as his brother stomped across the car park towards him.

'I'm fine. It's Beth. She's the one who's not.'

'Problems?'

'She's . . . in a mood this morning. Nothing I do is right,' he mumbled, reminding Joe of how he used to look when he was younger and had got into trouble at school for not doing his homework.

'But when you called and suggested coming up here this morning, I thought you said that Beth was OK about it? I wouldn't have agreed to come if I'd known — '

'She's fine,' Andrew cut in. 'Now, I've had enough talking for one morning. Which way up shall we go? I fancy the north ridge. What do you say?'

There was a touch of recklessness in his brother's eyes that made Joe uneasy. 'It could be tricky,' he said. 'You know how the ice can gather on that ridge. I fancy the west route. The sun's been on there for longer.'

12

'For pity's sake, Joe,' Andrew said as he hefted his rucksack onto his back and set off up the path, 'we've been climbing this route forever. I've had it up to here with playing safe. Let's live a little, shall we?' He looked back, a grin on his face, his eyes challenging. 'Of course, if it's too much for you, you only have to say and I'll do it on my own. How about it, old man? You losing your nerve?'

Joe laughed as he followed him along the stony track, boots crunching on the loose stones. 'Of course not. And not so much of the 'old', you cheeky beggar. Come on then. Let's make the most of this weather while it holds.'

Why did he let Andrew goad him like that? Why couldn't he have insisted on the west route? If only . . .

The climb was hard, as he'd known it was going to be: a scramble in places, slippery under foot in others. For a long time neither had any spare breath for conversation as they worked steadily towards the snow line, their breath misting in the crisp, cold air.

'Let's take a break,' Joe suggested after a while when they reached a rock big enough for them both to sit on. He took a flask of coffee from his rucksack, poured two cups and handed one to Andrew. They sat in silence for a while, watching a pair of buzzards wheeling across the sky, calling to each other.

'So,' Joe said quietly, hands wrapped around the cup as he inhaled the fragrant steam, 'want to tell me what's really bugging you?'

Andrew shook his head.

'Fair enough,' Joe said. 'But if you change your mind, it sometimes helps to talk about things, you know.'

Now why the hell did he say that? If only he'd just kept his big mouth shut. Why did he feel he had to push it?

'You want to know what's wrong?' Andrew said harshly, tossing the dregs of his coffee on to the short, spiky grass. 'OK, I'll tell you.'

It was like a cork being released from a bottle. Once he started talking about what it was that was eating him up inside, there was no stopping him. The angry, resentful words came tumbling out, fizzing and spitting. He was saying stupid, reckless things that, once he'd calmed down, he'd regret and apologise for. Joe knew this because that was Andrew's way. He'd sound off with lots of wild talk as he got it out of his system. Then, after a while, it would all calm down and they'd be able to talk it through. Calmly. Quietly. Sensibly.

Usually, Joe sat and waited for the storm to blow itself out. Why, then, did he have to do things differently that day? Andrew had been getting increasingly edgy lately, and Joe hoped it didn't mean what he feared it might. Was that why his brother had challenged him; told him, among other things, not to be so bloody childish?

'Well, what do you know?' Andrew said as he tossed the empty cup at Joe's feet and stood up. 'For once you and Beth agree about something. That's what she said.'

'Then she was right,' Joe muttered as he bent down to retrieve the cup.

Andrew gave a harsh laugh that hadn't a glimmer of humour in it. Only anger — burning, reckless, out of control. 'Know what else my wife said, bro? She said that she's fed up to the back teeth with you interfering in our lives all the time. And do you know what? So am I. So you can just butt out. Get yourself a life and stop trying to run mine.'

'Sit down and calm down, Andrew,' Joe said, struggling to keep his voice even and not let his own anger show.

But Andrew didn't sit down. He didn't calm down. Instead, he stomped off up the rough mountain path towards the ridge. He walked quickly and carelessly. Not the thing to do when you're part way up an icy mountain.

If only Joe hadn't interfered. Andrew was quite right about that. If only he'd just let his brother talk it out of his system and let him make his own decision about what he was going to do. If only he'd said he was busy that morning; that he had other things to do.

If only. Two such bloody useless words.

3

The village's tiny church was packed. But it could have been empty for all the notice I took. I walked alone, looking to neither left nor right, my eyes fixed intently on the spray of apricot roses in front of me. They rested on the top of Andrew's coffin and shook slightly as it swayed slowly along.

The roses had been my choice. Andrew didn't care for flowers. But I'd carried a bouquet of apricot roses on our wedding day, so it felt kind of appropriate.

I don't remember much about the service, only that it seemed to drag on forever. Hymns, prayers, more hymns, people saying what a great guy Andrew was, and even more damn hymns. Had I chosen them? And if so, why on earth had I chosen so many? I didn't remember doing so, but the last few days had passed in a blur.

But I did remember about the music, though. The vicar had asked me if I'd thought about having a piece of Andrew's favourite music played. But I'd shaken my head firmly. It was the only thing I was absolutely sure about.

For Andrew did, indeed, have a favourite piece of music. It dated back to his childhood, so he told me, when his mum and dad were still together. They'd been massive Queen fans and had sung along to their music every time they went anywhere in the car. Andrew's favourite was, without a doubt, 'Don't Stop Me Now', which he would belt out at the top of his lungs in the bath, in the car, whenever he was feeling particularly good about things. He even wanted it played at our wedding, but my mother had vetoed that, dismissing it as 'unsuitable'.

But to play it at his funeral? I shuddered. If it was unsuitable for a wedding, then it was a million times too upbeat and cheerful for a funeral. And there was no way on earth I could cope with hearing it. Not in a church full of people, most of whom were strangers to me. So I lied to the vicar and told her that, as far as I was aware, Andrew didn't have a favourite song. It was selfish, I know, but I promised myself that I'd play it for him when I was home. Blast it out. Fill the whole house, the entire valley even, with it.

For most of the service, as I sat beside my mother in the front pew. I kept my head bowed and stared down at my hands. They were clenched so tightly together that my wedding ring left marks on my fingers, but I didn't feel a thing.

Robot-like, I stood up when everyone else did. Sat down when they did. Bent my head at the appropriate times, although the only thing I was praying for was for it to be over.

And then it was. Almost. But there was worse to come.

As the pallbearers took up the coffin, I stood along with everyone else, feeling only a sense of relief that it would soon be over. But my relief was short-lived. Before I could move, the opening bars of a song I knew only too well rang out. 'Don't Stop Me Now' filled the church. Fast, furious party music.

I just wanted to get away from it, but I stumbled forward and would have fallen had my mother not reached out and pulled me towards her. I covered my mouth with my hands and wished I could cover my ears as well. I wanted to scream at someone to make it stop; to sink back down into the pew and not move until the music had finished and everyone had gone.

'Hang in there, darling. Hold it together just a little longer. Do it for Andrew.' My mother spoke quietly in my ear, her voice soothing yet strong. Then she put her arm around me and half-led, half-carried me out of the church and into the cold and wet November afternoon. We followed the coffin to a far corner of the tiny churchyard that looked down across the valley.

Andrew had taken me there one afternoon, not long after we'd bought Brackwith, to see where the Tennants had a family plot. He'd shown me his grandparents' and great-grandparents' names, and — a more recent addition — his father's.

'There are worse places to spend eternity,' he'd said, and we'd laughed and thought we had all the time in the world ahead of us before we needed to think about anything so morbid. Then we'd raced each other down to the pub, arriving laughing and breathless as we chased away any lingering shadows.

And now, the unthinkable. His name would be added to that list.

The short committal was, thankfully, soon over; and as I stepped away from the open grave, someone — I never knew who — put a hand on my shoulder and murmured that Andrew would be happy here, in the place he loved so much.

Happy? I whirled round, wanting to scream that if Andrew was happy, then damn him, he had no right to be.

Because I sure as hell wasn't.

But I checked myself. Just a little bit longer. I knew if I let the fury that was coiled up inside me spill out, it would never stop.

Then as I turned back, I saw him on the other side of the grave. Joe Tennant stood, leaning heavily on his crutches, his wheelchair just a couple of steps away. I thought he was still in hospital; I hadn't expected to see him there.

Was it you? I wanted to shout across at him. *Was it you who arranged to have that music played? Did you do it deliberately to hurt me? To punish me?*

But as he turned towards me, he looked so ashen-faced and ill that I felt a wave of pity for him. He'd loved and lost Andrew as well, and been terribly injured himself as he'd gone down to try and save him, or so I was told. I went to move towards him, to say something. But I stopped as I looked into his cold grey eyes and flinched.

Oh God, I thought. *He knows. Andrew must have told him.*

I stumbled away, only vaguely aware of my mother calling my name as she hurried after me. She caught up with me by the car and opened the door for me. A wake was to be held for Andrew in the village pub, and people were already drifting off down the hill towards it. I didn't even know who organised it, to be honest. Some of his climbing buddies, probably. But I couldn't face another person telling me what a great guy Andrew was, or how happy he'd be looking up at his beloved bloody mountains.

'Do you want to go to the pub, or shall I take you straight home?' Mum asked.

'Straight h-home, please.' My voice broke on the word 'home'. A home that still smelt of fresh primrose-yellow paint, and still had his clothes in the wardrobe, including those scruffy old jeans he used to wear for decorating. Still had his toothbrush in the bathroom and a half-read book on the cupboard by his side of the bed.

It didn't feel like home anymore. Not my home, anyway.

My mother was firmly of the 'bear up and get on with it' persuasion. She didn't do emotion, or allow anyone close enough to know how she was feeling. Not usually, anyway. But that day, as she turned towards me, her eyes glittered with unshed tears and there was a softness in her face I'd never seen before.

'I know, sweetheart, it's tough,' she said quietly. 'When I lost your father, it was like part of me had died with him. Which, in a way, it had. I thought I would never get over it.'

'Is this the bit where you tell me time is a great healer?' I said with a bitter edge to my voice. 'Because I've had it up to here with hearing that.'

'I know. And I wasn't going to tell you that. What I am going to say was that getting back to work helped. I had to carry on. For your sake.'

I didn't want to spoil the moment by

reminding her that, after my father died, I hardly saw her and spent the biggest part of my childhood being looked after by a series of childminders and after-school clubs while she was busy hauling herself up the corporate ladder. Her 'carry on for your sake' had never quite felt like that to me.

'Look, why don't you come back to London with me tomorrow?' she said as she eased her sleek top-of-the-range BMW carefully along the narrow road that snaked its way down to the valley bottom. 'You can't stay here on your own. It's not right. Your old room is still there, exactly as you left it.'

'I can't just walk away from the place,' I murmured. Although it was tempting. That half-finished book by the bed was breaking my heart. Not to mention the toothbrush and the parially eaten packet of biscuits that he loved and I hated. How was I going to deal with all that?

'Of course you can.' My mother's voice had reverted to its normal briskness now she was on safer, less emotional ground. 'You can come for a while, at least. Just to give yourself time to get your head together. Then, when you're feeling up to it, we'll come back here and I'll help you — you know, pack things away. Unless you'd like me to do it? Or, I'm sure we can arrange to get someone in.'

'No,' I said quickly. 'I'll do it. But not yet. I can't ... ' I let my voice trail away, and she drove in silence as she concentrated on easing her car up the rough stony track that led to Brackwith. But my mother doesn't do silence. At least, not for long.

'You know, I heard only yesterday that my company is about to recruit a fresh intake of accountancy trainees,' she said. 'I could put in a word for you. Maybe you could start studying again; pick up where you left off. You've got to look forward, Bethany. Keep busy. That's the way to get through this. Believe me, I know.'

'Mum,' I said quickly, once she'd

safely negotiated the unforgiving stone pillars at the entrance and parked the car safely. I didn't want the shock of what I was about to tell her to result in a very expensive dent in her very expensive car. 'There's no point in me going for something like that.'

'That's no way to talk. There's every point,' she said sharply, the uncharacteristic softness of a few moments ago long gone. 'You don't have to make any decisions on whether to sell the house yet. There are holiday property companies up here crying out to rent places with this sort of location. You should get more than enough income from it to cover your mortgage.'

'Yes, I know. But the thing is — '

'The thing is,' her mother steamrollered on in her best I-will-not-be-argued-with voice, 'You can't stay here on your own. Not at the moment. I wouldn't sleep another wink at the thought of it. So come along now. Pack a bag and we'll be off first thing in the morning. I'd like to make as early a start as possible. It's a long drive.'

She got out of the car and, with a yell of dismay, stepped straight into a large puddle. She cursed as her elegant — and, knowing my mother, ridiculously expensive — black suede court shoes turned the colour of pond sludge.

A wave of incredible weariness suddenly washed over me as I followed her muddy footprints into the house. I should have told her what I'd been holding back then; should have made her stop and listen to me. But I didn't. Instead, I actually fell asleep on the sofa while she was in the kitchen, trying to scrape the mud off her shoes before making us a cup of tea.

She found out the next morning, however, when she heard me throwing up in the bathroom. 'Oh my God,' she said when I emerged, white-faced and shaking, 'you're pregnant, aren't you?'

I nodded, not trusting myself to speak. Not trusting myself not to blurt out that it was the reason Andrew and I had rowed that last day. He'd accused me of getting pregnant deliberately; of trying to trap him. And — this was the bit that really stung — he said I'd pushed him into marriage, and now I was pushing him into parenthood before he was ready.

Was that what he'd told his brother? Was that why Joe had looked at me back there in the churchyard with hatred in his eyes? If Andrew had never met me, he would still be alive. Was that why Joe despised me?

'Well, that settles that,' my mother was saying firmly while I was still waiting for the churning sensation in my stomach to subside. 'You're coming home with me now while we sort out what we're going to do. There is no way on earth I'm going to let you stay a minute longer in this middle-of-nowhere place. Not in your condition.'

For the first time in my life, I didn't have the energy to argue with her, but stood and watched while she packed a few things for me, took me firmly by the arm and led me out of the house. I took one last backward look at the place that that once held all my happy-ever-after dreams. Then I looked up at the mountain that towered over it, the place where they had all ended.

'Don't look back,' my mother said. 'You need to start focusing on the future now, Bethany.'

The future? At that moment, I felt I had no future. But as my hand brushed across my stomach when I clicked the seat belt into place, I felt what I imagined was a baby bump, although of course it couldn't have been. It was way too early.

My heart lurched at the thought of it and I squeezed my eyes shut, as if by doing so I could shut out the panicky thoughts that bubbled up inside me. I was beyond tired. Exhausted. Wrung out.

And I never wanted to see Brackwith ever again.

4

Present day. Lake District.

'Thank you, Mr Horseface.'

My hands tightened on the steering wheel and my face began to burn as, for the tenth time in as many minutes, I relived one of the most cringe-making moments of my life — and believe me, there have been plenty. But this one had been off the scale of cringe-makingness, if there is such a word. And if there isn't, there should be.

I'd only gone and called Mr Hornsby (the bank manager, the man who held my financial future in his long, bony hands) Mr Horseface. The words whirred round and round inside my head like a hamster on a wheel. What on earth had I been thinking of? But the truth was, I hadn't been thinking, and that was the trouble. The words had slipped out before I could stop them. And I'd only realised what I'd said when I saw his dark bushy eyebrows shoot up in surprise.

A sudden bump on the left front wheel as it clipped a large stone that was on the side of the road jerked my attention back to my driving. The stone had fallen from the one of the walls that edged both sides of the narrow road as it wound its sinuous way along the valley bottom. Normally I drove this particular stretch very carefully, con-scious not only of the unforgiving nature of those stone walls but also the ever-present possibility of a couple of sheep or tourists that were often found ambling along in the middle of the road around the next blind bend. An unbudgeted bill for car repairs was the last thing I needed now that my careless tongue had ensured me a place in the 'not to be trusted with any more of the bank's money' category.

I stopped the car and checked for damage. As soon as I saw that I'd got away with it this time and there was no lasting damage, the hamster wheel inside my head started up again, even faster than before.

'Thank you, Mr Horseface.' For pity's sake, who in their right minds, on a grovelling mission to the bank manager, would risk blowing it by saying something so incredibly stupid?

It was because I'd been so nervous. I always blurt out the first thing that comes into my head when under stress. And, to be fair, his long, gloomy face did put me in mind of Pepper, the bad-tempered little pony my cousin Jen used to own when we were children. I used to spend huge chunks of the long school holidays on her father's farm while my mother was working.

Then there was the way Mr Horseface/ Hornsby had looked down that long, pointy nose at me like he'd just put his foot into something unpleasant. Or, I thought with a laugh quickly smothered, should that be his hoof? It had just made me even more nervous; even more likely to blurt out something stupid instead of my carefully rehearsed spiel about how Brackwith could be the best, most profitable guest house in the entire Lake District one day, provided he didn't carry out his threat to call in the overdraft and put me out of business.

I didn't tell him that Brackwith was more than just a house to me. It was the place that had saved my sanity; that had given me and my son a future. A place that meant more to me than anywhere else on earth. I figured he'd label me overly emotional, giving him one more reason to add me to that 'not to be trusted with the bank's money' list.

I glanced at my watch as I pulled up near the centre of the small lakeland village where Luke went to school. The gaggle of mums and buggies clustered around the entrance told me that, for the first time in the two years since Luke had started there, I was in fact early. Fifteen minutes early, to be precise. There was no way I wanted to hang around with the other mums, discussing the latest celebrity diet or whinging on about how their Kylie had been cast as a dancing banana in the forthcoming nativity play when everyone could see she'd make a perfect Angel Gabriel. Not today, when my Mr Horseface moment was still galloping around inside my head.

Goodness knows what I'd call Fiona Farrington-Smythe, the self-styled queen of the village. Not only was she president of the village's Women's Institute, organiser of the church flower rota and chair of the village hall committee, but she was also the lifelong best friend of Luke's teacher, the always-perfect and fount-of-all-knowledge Miss Doble.

I parked my car and headed up the nearly vertical lane that wound its way towards the village church. The squat grey stone building always put me in mind of a fat, broody hen, the way it hunkered down into the fell-side, looking as if it had grown out of some rocky outcrop rather than having been built by human hands.

I took a deep, steadying lungful of air and looked down across the valley. It was one of those glorious days that sometimes happen in November. The afternoon light accentuated the still-vivid colours of the last few leaves clinging stubbornly to the trees, while on the peaks at the head of the valley that same golden light glinted on the first snow patches of the year.

My thoughts winged back, as they often did on such a day, to the one seven years ago, almost to the day. The day when Andrew had gone out climbing, when he should have been home with me painting the sitting room walls Precious Primrose.

Time is a great healer, they told me, and although it's a cliché, it is nevertheless true. Up to a point. But for the rest of my life I will regret that stupid, petulant gesture when I turned my head away from his last goodbye kiss.

And even now, after all this time, it

still made my stomach lurch to see the headstone; to see the name 'Andrew William Tennant' in gold lettering underneath that of his father. It made it feel official somehow, which was daft because I knew he had gone. I'd built a life without him and moved on.

Yet for all that, it was still there, that old familiar coil of anger that rose to the surface whenever I came up here. Which was why I didn't do it as often as perhaps I should have done.

I turned to go. I shouldn't have come up here. It was a mistake, today of all days, when I was feeling so jangled. Better, surely, to have put up with the condescending remarks from Queen Fiona, who would no doubt lecture me on how I should expand my social life and stretch my mind by joining the WI's winter scrabble tournament. Or how I shouldn't bury myself away in that bleak back-of-beyond place of mine. Even the pitying looks from Fiona's little clique that always clustered around her like toadying courtiers would have been better than coming here and stirring up feelings that were best left buried. Or at least only uncovered when I was safely at home on my own.

I turned to go, then stopped abruptly as the churchyard gate opened with its usual rasping screech, and the last person in the world I wanted or expected to see stood there.

5

'Joe!' I whispered. I turned away, wondering if I could slip around the back of the church to avoid him, but it was too late. He'd already seen me.

I'd had a few stilted conversations with him on the phone over the years, but the last time I had actually seen him had been at Andrew's funeral. Leaning on his crutches, looking ashen-faced and ill, he'd been standing in the exact spot where I was standing now, one of his climbing buddies a discreet distance away with a wheel-chair.

But even though there was no sign of crutches or wheelchair now, he didn't look a lot better than he had that day. His face was thinner and free of bruises, his hair lightly flecked with grey, but the expression on his face as he saw me was as raw and angry as ever. He didn't have to speak. I could see from his face that he still blamed me for Andrew's death; still thought of me as — how had he so charmingly put it? 'A spoilt selfish brat who'd wanted it all and schemed and screamed until she got it.'

'Beth. I thought that was you,' he said in that clipped, carefully controlled voice I remembered so well. 'How are you?'

'I'm fine,' I muttered, wanting only to get away as quickly as possible. My prayer was answered when an eruption of noise from the village below indicated school had come out. 'Look, I'm sorry, but I really must dash. I'll be in all sorts of trouble with Luke's teacher if I'm late collecting him again. She's already got me lined up for her Bad Mother of the Year Award for the second year running.'

He gave a small, tight smile. 'I'm sure you're no such thing,' he said, although he didn't sound terribly convinced. 'And how is Luke?'

My voice warmed as it always did when I spoke of my son. 'Oh, he's fine. Just fine. Growing by the minute, which isn't surprising, given how much he eats. He never stops. He'll be taller than me before you know it.'

Shut up, Beth, I told myself. *Stop wittering and just go, before you say something you'll regret — for the second time today.*

And yet, for a moment, I was surprised to see a flicker of a smile across his thin face, a proper smile this time. A softening, too, of those cold grey eyes. The two brothers could not have been more different. Andrew had been warm, impulsive, always taking life at a gallop, while Joe was aloof and cold, with, according to Andrew, a stone for a heart and a calculator for a brain. A man who never did anything without carefully weighing up the odds.

Certainly Joe had a very sharp eye for business, and had taken on their parents' ailing hotel while still in his late teens. He was now the owner of a chain of very successful, very upmarket hotels. Most weekends, at least one of them would be featured in one of the Sunday supplements. He was, according to an article I'd read in one of those glossy magazines I only ever read at the hairdresser's, the intensely private owner of a business that specialised in taking run-down, ailing pubs and hotels and turning them around. He was, it reckoned, a man whose business was 'on trend and going places', whatever that meant. He was also, it concluded coyly, one of London's most confirmed bachelors.

'It sounds like Luke takes after his father,' Joe was saying while I was still woolgathering. 'When Andrew was a kid, I always used to think he had hollow legs, the amount of food he used to pack away. Either that, or he was feeding half the village — and, if I know my brother, charging them handsomely for the privilege.'

'That sounds like Andrew,' I said with a smile. Andrew was always looking for ways of making some easy money, preferably ones that didn't involve too much effort on his part.

'Look, I'm glad I've bumped into you, Beth,' Joe said suddenly as I turned to walk away. 'I was going to ring you. The thing is, I've got a present. For Luke.'

'Oh no, there's no need,' I said quickly. 'His birthday was ages ago, and besides, you're more than generous with his presents. He loved the Lego fire station, as I think he wrote and told you. And I always put the cash you send straight into his trust account, you know. For when he's older.'

You see? I wanted to say but didn't. *I can be a responsible mother. Not up to Miss Doble's impossibly high standards, of course. Nor yours, probably.*

'Well, this is nothing valuable, not in monetary terms anyway,' Joe said. 'It's an old train set Andrew used to enjoy playing with when he was about Luke's age. It used to keep him happy for hours. I've got it with me in the car. I thought perhaps I could bring it up?'

Joe, come to Brackwith? I felt a whirl of panic spiral up inside me. Why would he want to do that? He hadn't set foot inside the place since Andrew's death, or expressed any interest in doing so. Why now?

I took a step backward as I remembered the last time he'd been at Brackwith. It was not long after Andrew and I had moved in, about three months before Andrew's death. How angry he'd been with the pair of us. Scathing about how foolish we were to take on such a large mortgage without talking to him first, or at least getting a proper survey done before committing ourselves. A money pit, that's what he'd called the rambling old house and neglected farm buildings. It was, he assured us, going to come crumbling down around our ears sooner or later.

Well, he wasn't wrong there.

For years, I'd dreamed of proving him wrong. It was one of the things that had kept me going through some pretty dark times. But there was no chance of that at the moment. I couldn't let him see the house in the state it was. Couldn't bear to see his face as he saw the leaking roof and rotting window frames. I shrank from giving him the opportunity of saying 'I told you so.' Perhaps next year, when the roof had been fixed? No, I couldn't cope with it today.

'Well, the thing is, I — we're a bit busy at the moment,' I stammered, as my face began to burn. 'Perhaps another time?'

I took a step back, dragged my hand through my hair like I do when I'm a flustered, and quite forgot that it was still scraped back into the tightly wound bun I'd forced it into in a pathetic — and totally futile — attempt to impress the unimpressible Mr Horse-face. A shower of hairpins flew out and hit the stone path with a melodic tinkle.

Joe went to pick them up but I shook my head and hurried past him. 'It's all right. Leave them,' I said quickly.

'Look, I've got to go. Sorry, Joe. If I'm late . . . '

I scurried away, like a mouse who's just come eyeball to eyeball with a hungry cat. Running away? Too right I was. I'd already sat through one lecture that day about where I was going wrong with my life. I'd had no choice but to take it from Mr Horseface, but I sure as heck wasn't in the mood to take another one from Joe.

No, it was out of the question. There was no way he could come to Brackwith. Maybe I could arrange for Luke to meet him in Ambleside, or at his hotel?

But I'd only got as far as the churchyard's squeaky gate before my conscience kicked in. What was I thinking of? Of course Luke would love to have something that belonged to his father. Especially a train set. I'd no right denying him that.

And I should have invited Joe to Brackwith, to meet Luke. After all, apart from my mother, he was his only living relative. I'd no right to stop him visiting Luke. And if he didn't like what he saw at Brackwith, well, that was just too bad. I'd put up with his disapproval, for Luke's sake.

I turned back but saw that he was kneeling in front of Andrew's grave. Was he praying? I didn't know. Whatever it was, I decided it was best not to interrupt him. And I really was going to be late collecting Luke if I hung around any longer.

I'd invite him another time, I decided. That would give me time to work out what to say to him, something I was no nearer doing than I had been seven years ago. After all, what words are there? How do you say 'I'm sorry I caused your brother's death'?

6

'Damn it to hell!' Joe cursed as he bent down to pick up the hairpins from the path and felt his knee give way so that he stumbled forward, his bad leg locked at an impossibly awkward angle as it sometimes did. He dropped forward onto his knees in an attempt to free it and hoped Beth hadn't looked back. The last thing he wanted was for her to come rushing across to see if he needed help.

After what seemed forever, he was eventually able to straighten up again, but only by putting his hand out towards Andrew's headstone for support. He bit his lip hard as he fought the pain. His left leg was as bad as ever today, probably not helped by the climb up the nearly vertical lane that led to the churchyard.

This was the first time he'd been

back here since Andrew's funeral, and he'd forgotten how steep the lane was. But even if he had remembered, he'd have still come. Except now that he was here, he wondered why. Andrew wasn't here, in this neatly tended graveyard. If his spirit lived on anywhere, it would be up there on the wild, windswept mountains. He looked up to where the brooding mass of Brackwith Fell towered above the valley, casting its long shadow, even on a bright sunny day like today. He looked quickly away as the memories rushed back, and instead forced his mind back to the present.

What a shock it had been to see Beth standing here by the grave. And yet, of course, why wouldn't she? He'd hoped she would have moved on by now, and built a life for herself and Luke. Yet her face still had the same haunted, empty look that she'd had at the funeral. And, then as now, she'd been unable to bring herself to look at him. Was she still grieving for Andrew, after all this time?

Did she still . . .

'It's Joe, isn't it? Joe Tennant. It's so good to see you back.'

Joe turned to see the vicar approaching him. 'It's just a flying visit,' he said as he desperately tried but failed to remember the woman's name. 'I was up this way on business, so thought I'd take a detour. So here I am.'

'And you'll be looking in on Beth and Luke, no doubt.' The vicar smiled. 'My word, but he's getting to be the image of his dad, isn't he? And such a lovely boy. He's a real credit to Beth.'

Joe twisted the hairpin between his fingers, then winced as it bit into his palm. 'He is, isn't he?' he said, not wanting to admit that the only images he had of Luke were from the photographs, mostly school ones, that Beth dutifully sent every birthday and Christmas along with a polite but rather formal thank-you note.

'Look, I'm sorry,' the vicar went on. 'I've got a class in five minutes, otherwise I'd have invited you back to the vicarage for a cup of tea and a chat. Are you staying long?'

'Sadly, no. Like I said, this is just a flying visit. I've got to be back in London tomorrow.'

'Well, I'm sure Beth and Luke will be delighted to see you. No doubt I'll hear all about your visit from Luke at Sunday school.' She gave him a warm smile and went inside the church.

Joe thought back to the way Beth had backed away from him at his suggestion that he come up to Brackwith to deliver the train set in person to Luke. Yeah, right. She'd looked just about delighted as a chicken who'd wandered into a fox's den by mistake.

It was hard to remember what she'd been like before Andrew died. She was still as lovely as ever, of course; still had those same startling green eyes that looked as if they could see into your very soul. Still had that wild red hair that she used to wear loose. He was not sure the new, more severe hairstyle suited her, but he was glad to see she hadn't changed the colour as well. But, of course, *she* would have changed. Being a widowed single mother would have seen to that. She was no longer the carefree, bubbly young woman she'd been back when Andrew had first brought her home to meet him.

Joe had never thought Andrew would settle with a steady girlfriend, as he'd always been a 'love them and leave them' type of guy. But Beth, he guessed, had not been so easy to leave. The one to finally tie down his wouldn't-be-tied brother. To say he'd been astonished when Andrew had announced he and Beth were getting married was an under-statement, although he pretty soon realised that Beth seemed a lot keener on the idea than Andrew.

Nevertheless, Andrew seemed quite happy to go along with it, even when Beth's mother managed to turn the whole thing into a big production number. Goodness knew, he'd have thought the money would have been better spent on the young couple's house than designer dresses and a no-expense-spared wedding in one of the priciest lakeside hotels in the area. An astute and highly successful businesswoman, Helen Garrett had managed to combine her daughter's wedding with an opportunity to further her career by inviting more business acquaintances than friends and family. The whole event had been more like a corporate function than a wedding.

Not that Beth and Andrew appeared to care. They were like a couple of young kids playing at house. But then, Joe thought wryly, they were in fact little more than kids at the time. Beth had some money left her by her late father; and when, after they'd been married a couple of years, they found and fell in love with Brackwith, this great barn of a place partway up Brackwith Fell, Beth was determined to buy it. It was, Joe had told them, a money pit, and most unsuitable for a pair of first-time buyers, particularly ones who were foolish enough not to get a proper survey done before signing on the dotted line. But by the time he knew about it, it was too late; they'd already signed the contract. And even if he had known, nothing he or Helen Garrett — and for once, the two of them had finally found something they could agree on — said could change their minds.

He shook his head sadly at the memory of that spirited, confident girl she'd been. Back then nothing had frightened her, least of all Joe. She'd been infuriating, yes. Headstrong and determined, not to mention utterly convinced that she knew what she was doing when it was patently obvious she didn't. But that was before seven years of single parenthood, not to mention the desperate struggle she must have had to keep Brackwith going. When he'd first heard that she'd gone back to London with her mother after the funeral, Joe never thought she would be back. But he was wrong. He admired her guts for the way she'd stuck at it — but at what cost to herself?

Poor girl, he thought as the sounds of children's voices drifted up to him. She'd looked frightened to death, and couldn't get away from him fast enough. She'd beetled off down the hill as if scared he would come running after her. Maybe she'd have been less anxious if she'd realised that his running days were well and truly over.

He took out his phone and dialled. It was so long before it was answered that he was about to give up when a breathless voice said hello.

'I'm sorry,' he said, 'you sound out of breath. It's just . . . I've just bumped into Beth. In the churchyard of all places. I don't know which one of us was the most surprised. I was just wondering if there's been any more movement on the house-selling front. Is she up for it, do you think? Has she said anything to you?'

He turned the hairpins over in his hand as he listened to the voice on the other end. 'Right. And you don't know how it went? Anyway, just to let you know, I tried to wangle an invite up to Brackwith, but she wasn't having it. She just looked at me like I'd suggested selling her into slavery and scurried away. So I've sort of scuppered my plan to just turn up there unannounced with some stuff I've got for Luke. I must admit, I wasn't expecting an outright refusal like that. I'll have to have a think about where I go from here now. I'll let you know.'

Where do *I go from here?* he asked himself as he ended the call. Clean out of ideas with nowhere to go, that was where. He'd tried. Maybe it was time to get in the car and go home. There was nothing here for him.

He took one last look at his brother's grave and limped away, his leg hurting more than it had in a long time. But before he reached the car, his phone rang. He took it out and blinked in surprise when he saw who the caller was.

7

During the drive home, Luke kept up a constant stream of chatter about who'd done what to whom during break, interspersed with the latest pronouncements from the all-seeing, all knowing Miss Doble who was, it seemed, the authority on everything from the toilet habits of the ancient Egyptians to the behavioural problems of ferrets.

I wondered what Miss Doble would say about people who refused basic hospitality to their brothers-in-law, or insulted their bank managers by calling them silly names. I could probably guess. Little Miss Perfect Doble was a neat, colour-coordinated woman who probably wore matching underwear and would never dream of going to bed without first cleansing, toning and moisturising. I counted it a good day if I could find matching socks, never mind underwear. My hair was in a permanent state of rebellion, and I could never manage to send Luke off to school with the right piece of kit, book or form duly signed. In Miss Doble's eyes I was, without doubt, A Bad Mother. And a beyond-bad sister-in-law.

Yep. As bad days went, this was turning out to be way up there with the worst of them. Well, not the worst of them, obviously. When you've had a sombre-faced policeman knocking on your door, nothing gets worse than that. But this one was certainly near the top of the 'could have been better' league.

I eased the car up the rough stone track and turned into what used to be the farm entrance. The house was snuggled up against the fell-side, its small white-framed windows sparkling like precious gems against the slate-grey walls as they reflected the setting sun. But for once not even that sight could soothe my jangled nerves. For the first time, I was seeing it through Joe's eyes; seeing what he would have seen if I'd agreed to him coming up here. The leaking roof. The rotting window frames. The warped back door that never closed properly. The money pit.

I forced myself to face the unthinkable. What would I do if I had to leave the place as the Brittons had before me? Centuries of farming at Brackwith had ended twelve years earlier with the death of Ted Britton, the old farmer. The family had scraped a living of sorts off the farm for hundreds of years, but his children and grandchildren had no interest in the precarious and hard life of a Cumbrian hill farmer. I didn't blame them, of course, but I always felt a tug of sadness every time I went into the barn where, even after all these years, the warm, sweet scent of hay and cattle still lingered. Old Mrs Britton had struggled on alone in the house she'd come to as a young bride, but it became too much for her, so she sold the livestock and gradually the place fell into disrepair.

But the house itself was sound

enough, built squat and low into the side of the fell, protection against the winter storms that rampaged across the fell tops and screamed down through the valleys. Its thick stone walls kept its occupants warm in the winter and cool in the summer, as it had done for hundreds of years.

When Andrew and I first bought it, just months before he died, it was run-down and neglected. It had been a long, hard struggle to turn it from that to the warm, cosy home it was today — give or take the odd leaky roof, rotting window frames and that wretched back door that only closed properly if you knew the exact spot to apply a well-aimed kick.

But I'd always reckoned, however hard it was, that it was worth all the effort, all the money my father had left me, even the grovelling to Mr Horseface, to keep things together. To give Luke the sort of childhood home neither Andrew nor I had had. I figured I owed his memory that.

But now thanks to my moment of sheer insanity in the bank and my less-than-impressive profit forecast that I'd stayed up half the night working on (not to mention the 'sensible-looking' bun I'd forced my hair into), it was all for nothing.

'But it won't come to that,' I muttered with fierce determination as I backed the car into the space behind the old dairy. 'I simply won't let it. I'll do whatever it takes, even if I have to get up on that wretched roof myself.'

'Can I come up on the roof with you, Mummy?' Luke asked as I realised I'd spoken my thoughts aloud.

'No, of course not. I didn't really mean I was going to go up on the roof.'

'But you said — '

'Sometimes, Luke, grown-ups say things they don't really mean.'

'You mean, like telling fibs?' His voice rose in squeaky indignation. 'But — but, Mummy, you said we shouldn't tell fibs. You said — '

'I know, I know. And usually that's

true, of course. But — look, why don't you go and see where Mrs Biscuit is? I think she said something about doing some baking today. Go round the back. It'll take me forever to find my front door key.'

I let Luke out of the car and he raced ahead, whooping with excitement and in through the ever-open back door. He charged along the long passageway, ignoring the room where we kept coats and outdoor boots and shoes, and headed straight into the kitchen, where the warm smell of baking had his nose twitching like a bloodhound on the scent.

I followed him, laden down with school bags, coats and my briefcase. I promised myself to go back later, once I'd dumped everything, and kick the door shut. But first I needed a sit-down, a change of shoes and twenty-four hours of uninterrupted sleep. Although not necessarily in that order.

I wished I had half of Luke's energy

63

— not to mention his appetite, as I realised with a jolt of surprise that, in all the rushing around I'd been doing that day, I'd completely forgotten to have lunch. As we walked into the kitchen, Mrs Biscuit looked up from the pastry she was rolling out and beamed at us both.

And that was another thing that was constantly niggling away at the back of my mind. Mrs Biscuit, bless her, was the sole reason I was still in business, even if I was merely hanging on by my fingertips or, in bank-manager speak, walking a very fine tightrope between survival and bankruptcy.

Shocked and disorientated after Andrew's death, I'd gone back to London to stay with my mother; but it hadn't worked out, particularly once Luke was born. She had never really taken to motherhood herself, and had kept the promise she'd made the day I was born that she would never, ever go through that again. Any hopes I might have harboured about how becoming a grandmother might finally trigger her missing maternal streak were quickly dashed. She bit her lip so hard and so often every time Luke so much as whimpered that for the sake of her sanity — and her lips — I finally packed up my tiny son and brought him back to Brackwith, to the life I'd originally planned for him.

Except, of course, for the dead father bit. That had never been part of the plan.

★　★　★

Much against my mother's advice ('throwing good money after bad' was her constant mantra at that time), I'd used some of the money Dad had left me to get the mortgage down to slightly more manageable proportions and to get the rooms up to letting standard. Within weeks of opening as Brackwith Farm Guest House, the bookings started coming in, and things were looking promising. I'd always had an eye for interior design and, with a minimum of spend and the maximum ingenuity, managed to turn the draughty old farmhouse into a warm and welcoming home with fresh flowers in every room and crisp, lavender-scented linen on the beds. Everything looked and smelt good. The guests liked the location, the rooms, the beds, the views from the windows. Everything, they said, was brilliant.

Everything, that was, except the cooking. Which was unfortunate, because when you're in the bed and breakfast business, the breakfast bit is every bit as important as the bed bit; and Andrew used to say — with some justification — that I was to cooking what Victoria Beckham was to sumo wrestling. What, then, had I been thinking of, running a guest house when I couldn't boil an egg, least of all offer my unfortunate guests the choice of boiled, scrambled or fried?

Because the cooking was never supposed to be down to me, that's why. That was going to be Andrew's job.

He'd grown up in the hotel trade and was a good, if spectacularly messy, cook who always lost interest by the time it came to do the washing-up.

So I used a bit more of my father's money to pay a woman called Sally to come in to do the cooking for me, while I did everything else, which was fine. Things bobbed along reasonably well until about six months ago, when the money ran out and I had to let Sally go. I muddled on as best I could until a guest we called Mrs Biscuit arrived. She took one horrified look at my under-cooked bacon and overcooked eggs, went into the kitchen and cooked not only her own breakfast but mine and Luke's as well. And to my everlasting surprise and relief, she has been with us ever since. She was, she told me, a recently retired professional cook who was at a loose end and was only too happy to hang around. And no, she didn't want any money. Just room and board for as long as she chose to stay.

Of course, her name wasn't really

Mrs Biscuit. It was Ivy Biston, but Luke called her Mrs Biscuit and the name stuck. It suited her, with her sweet dumpling face, little currant eyes and the fragrance of cinnamon and lemons that clung to her like a cloak. Luke adored her. So, too, did I. But there was hardly a day went by when I didn't worry about how on earth I'd manage if — or, more likely, when — Mrs Biscuit decided to leave as suddenly as she'd appeared.

'I'm starving,' Luke said plaintively. 'I didn't have hardly anything for lunch.'

'Oh dear. Well, there are some Brussels sprouts and broccoli left over from last night,' Mrs Biscuit said, then chuckled at his dismayed expression. 'Or almond slices, still warm from the oven. Which will it be?'

As she handed Luke an almond slice, she offered me one and gave a small anxious frown when I shook my head. 'Things didn't go so well in the bank, then?' she asked sympathetically.

'The bank?' I looked at her blankly

for a few seconds, as my conscience, which I'd been trying to ignore during the drive home, finally caught up with me. Whatever had gone on in the past, Joe was still Andrew's brother, and had been very good to us when we'd first married. He'd bailed us out financially on more than one occasion. I'd no right denying him the chance to meet Luke, had I? Not now he'd expressed an interest in doing so. Until now, I'd always assumed he didn't want to know, and certainly he'd made no mention of wanting to see us before. So why now? What had changed his mind?

Mrs Biscuit tapped the plate of cakes. 'Hello? Earth to Beth,' she said in a voice that set Luke giggling.

'Sorry,' I said. 'I was miles away. What were you saying?'

'I was asking about your visit to the bank?' I must have still looked like I was away with the fairies, because she went on: 'You know, that place where the bosses pay themselves obscene bonuses while at the same time pushing their customers to the point of bankruptcy by calling in their loans.' In Mrs Biscuit's view, bankers were just one tiny step up from the things that squelched about on the bottom of muddy ponds.

'Oh yes, the bank. I'm sorry, I'd forgotten I hadn't brought you up to speed on that. Seeing Joe has really thrown me. It's just . . . well, I wasn't expecting to see him. Especially not there in the churchyard. It was a shock.'

'Joe?' Mrs Biscuit's busy hands stilled for a moment.

'Of course, I keep forgetting you don't know him. Joe is Andrew's older brother. They were out climbing together when Andrew . . . when he had the accident. He works down south somewhere, London I think. He doesn't come up here very often. We — we're not very good at staying in touch, though he never forgets Luke's birthdays or Christmas. He's very . . . ' I struggled for the right word. 'Very conscientious,' was the best I could come up with.

'He bought me a Lego fire station for my birthday,' Luke said between mouthfuls of almond slice. 'With a fire engine and a helicopter. It's awesome.'

'I don't even know how long he's up here for,' I said. 'I was in a hurry to pick Luke up, so I'm afraid there wasn't much time for social pleasantries.' I omitted to add that even if we'd had all the time in the world, there still wouldn't have been much of an exchange of pleasantries between us.

'And is he coming here?' Mrs Biscuit asked as she bent her head over the mixing bowl.

I shook my head. 'I feel really bad now that I didn't invite him. But then again, he didn't bother to tell me he was coming, so I daresay he wouldn't even have thought about coming to see me if we hadn't bumped into each other in the churchyard. He looked as shocked to see me as I was to see him. Oh, but hang on — that's not right, because he said he had some things of Andrew's, some toys that he thought

Luke might like. So he must have intended to come up here to see us, mustn't he?'

'Something for me?' Luke's face lit up. 'I hope it's more Lego. When's he coming?'

'I don't know. I — I left things a bit . . . sort of vague.' I could feel my face getting hotter as I relived the moment when I'd all but told Joe not to come. And once again, hot shame washed over me. 'Look, I'll just give him a call. I've got his number here somewhere. He always puts it on Luke's cards, which I never throw away. They're in the dresser drawer somewhere. And Luke, while I'm finding it, you go on upstairs and change out of your school clothes.'

'But Mummy — '

'Now,' I said in my sternest voice, and winced as he stomped up the stairs, his footsteps sounding like a herd of wildebeest stampeding through the house.

'This Joe — you say he's not been here before?' Mrs Biscuit asked. 'Not in all the time you've lived here?'

'Not since Andrew died. It's just . . . well, we don't really get on. He never approved of me and Andrew. Made no secret of the fact that he thought we were too young to get married, which I suppose with hindsight we were. And as for buying this place, there was the most almighty row about it because he didn't approve, and . . . well, you know how it is. Things got said, and then there was Andrew's accident. And Joe hasn't been here since. No reason to come, I suppose.' As I spoke, I was rifling through the drawer. 'Yes, there it is. Now, if you'll excuse me, I'd better get it over with.' *Before I lose my nerve*, I could have added, but didn't. I didn't even give myself time to think about what I was going to say.

'Oh Joe, I'm so glad I caught you,' I said quickly when he answered. 'Look, I'm sorry about earlier. It was . . . well, seeing you like that, it was a bit of a shock, and . . . well, what must you have thought of me? Luke would love to meet you. How long are you staying up here for?'

'I'm going back tomorrow,' he said. 'An important meeting I can't get out of.'

'OK.' I took a deep breath. 'Well, how about now? You'll have to take us as you find us, mind. And the place is a bit at sixes and sevens because we thought we were having builders in this week. But now we're not, and — '

'Now will be absolutely fine. I'll see you in about half an hour then. And, Beth?'

'Yes?'

'Thank you,' he said with such obvious sincerity it made me feel a million times worse.

8

Luke came back as I finished the call and cast longing glances at the almond slices cooling on the rack.

'OK. Just one more,' I said. 'But then that's enough, otherwise you won't eat your supper, and it looks like Mrs Biscuit is making your favourite pie.'

'Chicken and bacon?' His face lit up.

'Brussel sprouts and broccoli,' said Mrs Biscuit, laughing at Luke's horrified face as she turned back to me. 'Is he coming?' she asked me.

I nodded, trying to make my voice sound cooler than I felt. 'In about half an hour.'

'Right then. I'll make myself scarce when he does. You'll have things to talk about.'

My heart lurched. 'Oh no, please don't do that. I — it'll be easier if you're there.'

'Easier?' Mrs Biscuit gave me a sharp look. 'You're making him sound like — ' She broke off as she saw Luke watching her with undisguised interest. 'So, changing the subject for a moment, you still haven't told me how it went with the bank. Did they get the thumbscrews out?'

'What's a thumbscrew?' Luke asked. 'Is it to screw your thumbs on if they fall off?'

'Something like that, pet,' Mrs Biscuit answered, then looked across at me. 'Well? Did they?'

'Not quite. Actually, it all got a bit awkward.' I squirmed at the memory of the 'Mr Horseface' moment. But there was no way I was going to admit to that, certainly not in front of Luke. 'He wasn't terribly impressed with my cash flow projection and budget forecast. I was being 'overly optimistic', I think was how he put it. But at least he didn't call in the overdraft, which was something to be thankful for. He said that for the moment there are sufficient funds, whatever he meant by that. I imagine Mum must have taken pity on my last desperate plea and put some cash into my account, even though she'd said something about hell freezing over before she'd throw more good money after bad again. I'll phone her later.'

'And the loan for the roof — did he go for that?' Mrs Biscuit asked gently.

I shook my head. 'A big fat no. Didn't even pretend to consider it. He said it wasn't a sound enough business proposition and that the tourist trade is notoriously fickle. It would, he said, be gambling with the bank's money, which he was not inclined to do. So that's it. Goodness only knows what we're going to do now, short of going up on the roof and doing it myself.'

Mrs Biscuit's round face crumpled. 'Oh, I'm so sorry, pet. That means Room Three out of use for the winter then?'

I'd had to put the builder, due to start work on the leaky roof this week, on hold when he found something very nasty and very, very expensive in the roof timbers in that part of the house.

'Unless we don't get any rain or snow between now and next April, yes. Maybe in the spring when the bookings start picking up again, I can scrape together the necessary money. But it had to be our most popular room, didn't it?' Room Three had the best view in the house, looking as it did down across the valley and up to the stark, rocky outline of Brackwith Pike. It used to be my and Andrew's room, but since his death I preferred the one at the back of the house that looked not at the mountain but instead across what in Ted Britton's time had been the cattle-collecting yard.

I dragged my hand through my hair, and as I did so the last of the hairpins, which I'd been shedding steadily ever since leaving the bank, slid out of my hair and chinked onto the floor. In my desperation to appear the kind of trustworthy customer the bank would be happy to lend their money to (think Miss Doble, without the matching underwear), I'd used an entire packet of pins and half a gallon of hairspray trying to fool my hair into looking like a sleek orderly bun for once, instead of what on my worst bad-hair days always reminded me of an unravelling Brillo Pad. I'd even bought myself this fancy leather briefcase for £2.50 from a charity shop in Kendal. It weighed a ton and had so many different flaps and pockets that I kept losing things. But I reckoned it made me look businesslike and capable.

Businesslike and capable? Who am I kidding? I thought as a rush of despair engulfed me. The hair, the briefcase, the neatly typed profit forecast — it was all nothing but a sham. The fact that I was still in business was solely down to Mrs Biscuit. Before she appeared like Superman (but more amply proportioned and without the tights), my business was going downhill faster than a runaway carthorse. And when she moved on, as she was bound to do eventually, the downward gallop would start all over again — and this time no one would be able to stop it.

Mrs Biscuit handed me a mug of tea. 'Here. This'll make you feel better, pet.'

I took the steaming mug with a weak smile. Right now, the only thing that would really make me feel better would be a nice big win on the lottery, which was not going to happen seeing as I'd never bought a lottery ticket in my life. Maybe it was time I started.

'Melissa Stanley was sick all down her skirt and in her shoes in the playground after lunch,' Luke said as he wolfed down his almond slice. 'I told her she shouldn't hang upside-down on the bars straight after eating, but she still did it and then she was sick. And, Mummy, you said you'd put my school trip form in my bag, but you didn't. I emptied my bag on the table and Miss Doble said 'Oh Luke, not again', and that it's got to be in tomorrow or else.'

My pointed comment that as far as I

was aware, there wasn't about to be a world shortage of almond slices and that he should therefore take his time eating, died on my lips as I remembered the other cringe-making moment in the bank. I'd been trying to put the 'Horseface' moment behind me as I'd fumbled among the many sections and pockets in the briefcase for what I thought was this dead impressive profit forecast, the one I'd been up half the night working on. I found, instead, a custard-yellow form. It was headed 'Year 2 Trip to Coniston'.

Of course, I should have explained to Luke how in the panic of getting him off to school and the upcoming meeting with the bank hanging over my head like a storm cloud, the form had somehow ended up by mistake in my briefcase instead of his bag. That is, after all, what Good Mothers would do. A Good Mother would never try to fob her children off with something that, while not exactly a lie, was not exactly the truth either. No wonder he looked sceptical when I mumbled something about how the form would probably turn up sooner or later.

Miss Doble was, as always, right, I thought wearily as I sipped my tea. I was not A Good Mother. I was a ditzy, muddle-headed mother of a son who was six going on forty-six and was far more sensible than me. More sensible, probably, than Mr Hornsby — and certainly a whole lot nicer. I often wondered how Andrew (who'd been even less sensible than me) and I had produced a child like Luke. Sometimes I wondered if there'd been a mix-up at the hospital when he was born. But then I'd see Andrew's piercing blue eyes laughing up at me from Luke's face. And the poor child had certainly inherited my wild carroty hair that defied gravity and contrived to grow in six different directions.

My mother, who planned, managed and organised every aspect of her own life, had put in her cosmic order when she was expecting me for a dainty Miss

Doble-type little girl. In other words, a miniature version of herself. But the heavens must have lined up wrong that night, because instead she got me. And although she loved me — and was absolutely brilliant the way she carried me through those first terrible months after Andrew died — she never really forgave the universe for the mix-up. Or my father's side of the family for passing on to me the long, gangly limbs and the unruly carroty hair. And she certainly never forgave my father for succumbing to a fatal heart attack when I was 11 years old, leaving her to carry on battling up the corporate ladder much as before — but leaving me without the one person in my young life who'd made time to talk to me.

She didn't approve of Mrs Biscuit either. They'd met a few weeks ago when Mum arrived for what I always thought of as her annual inspection — of me, the house and Luke. We all failed, of course, as we did every year. But Mrs Biscuit's failure to come up to

Mum's impossibly high standards was legendary, and still made me giggle whenever I recalled the moment when Mrs Biscuit had pushed a wodge of chocolate fudge cake at Mum, who was stick-thin and fiercely determined to stay that way, and advised her to 'get some meat on your bones'.

'. . . so I told him to call back later. What is it with you today, Beth? You were away with the fairies again.' I became aware of Mrs Biscuit looking closely at me, her round face creased with worry. 'Is there something else bothering you, pet?'

'No, I'm just tired, that's all. I didn't get much sleep last night, worrying about the meeting with the bank. Sorry, who did you tell to come back later?'

'That lanky rasher of wind who's forever hanging around like a bad smell.' Mrs Biscuit sniffed. 'Never trust a man with sandy eyelashes, that's what I always say.'

'What's a rasher of wind?' Luke wanted to know. 'I know what a rasher of bacon is, but how can you have a rasher of wind?'

'Luke, don't you have some reading practice to do? Go and get your bag.' I made a mental note to ask Mrs Biscuit to be more careful what she said in front of him. Otherwise, next time he saw Simon, a local estate agent I'd been seeing quite a lot of recently, he'd call him Mr Rasher-of-Wind. Or worse. But then, who was I to lecture anyone on inappropriate names?

'What did Simon want?' I asked. 'Did he say?'

Mrs Biscuit shook her head. 'Of course not. He's hardly likely to entrust that sort of information to an underling like me.'

'Oh, for heaven's sake, he's not like that,' I said.

'How do you know?' Mrs Biscuit's face was suddenly grave. 'Seriously, pet, what do you know about him?'

'I know he was a friend of Andrew's; that they went to the same school together,' I said. Though to be honest, I couldn't remember Andrew ever talking about a friend called Simon. But then again, our time together had been so brief — just one month short of two years — that I was finding it harder than ever to remember everything about him.

'Oh yes — and while you were out charming bank managers,' Mrs Biscuit went on, 'I took a call from the Turners, confirming their booking for next week. I've left the details on the dresser for you. And Mr Lawrence is going out this evening and asked if he could have his supper early.'

Mr Lawrence, a retired teacher and enthusiastic bird-watcher from Manchester, was another of those guests who, like Mrs Biscuit, came for a week and was still here, months later. Though I reckoned in his case the attraction was Mrs Biscuit's cooking, or maybe even Mrs Biscuit herself, if the way his eyes twinkled when he looked at her was anything to go by.

'You know, these evening meals . . . '

I said. 'You shouldn't be doing them for the guests. It's a terrible tie.'

'And what else would I be doing with my evenings?' Mrs Biscuit snorted. 'Talking of which, the rasher of wind said to tell you — '

'Little pitchers,' I warned, looking at Luke. 'And, Luke, if you gave the same level of concentration to your reading practice as you do to earwigging conversations that are nothing to do with you, you'd be halfway through *War and Peace* by now.'

'What's *War and Peace*?'

But before I could explain, there was a rap at the kitchen door and the 'rasher of wind' himself stood there. And, judging from the expression on his face, he'd heard every word.

9

'I did knock,' he said, 'but as the back door was open, I came on in when nobody heard me. I hope you don't mind?'

'Mind? No, of course not,' I said. I did in fact mind, but was too flustered by his sudden appearance, and the worry of whether or not he'd overheard Mrs Biscuit's less-than-complimentary description of him, to make anything of it. 'I left the door open when Luke and I came in and meant to go back and shut it.'

'Which I have now done,' he said, giving me a stern look. 'You really should be more security-conscious, you know, Beth, living in such an isolated spot.'

I flushed. It seemed to be my day for getting lectured. Time for a swift change of subject, I reckoned. 'Mrs

Biscuit was just telling me that you'd phoned.'

'So I heard,' he said with a scowl at Mrs Biscuit, who looked back at him with an expression of injured innocence more often seen on a rugby pitch and usually followed by the words, 'Who? Me, ref? I was nowhere near him.'

'But you shouldn't have dragged yourself all the way up here,' I went on quickly before Mrs Biscuit or Luke could make things any worse, especially when the poor man had taken the trouble to make the thirty-minute drive from his office in town up to Brackwith. 'Especially when I know how busy you are at the moment. Why didn't you just phone and leave a message?'

'Because I've got some great news for you, Beth.' His face was suddenly lit up by a brilliant smile. 'And I wanted to deliver it to you in person.'

'Well I could really do with some good news at the moment,' I said with feeling. 'So what is it?'

'Can we talk in private?' he said,

nodding at Mrs Biscuit and Luke, who were both watching us with undisguised interest.

'Mrs Biscuit, would you mind taking Luke into the sitting room? Perhaps you'd be kind enough to listen to his reading practice?' I looked at her pleadingly. I'd prefer to hear whatever Simon had to say here in the kitchen. The last time he'd been in the sitting room, he'd made a point of commenting on my wedding photo that still took pride of place on the old out-of-tune piano I'd inherited with the house. Maybe, he'd hinted, it was time I moved on. Which I had done. I'd always miss Andrew and regret what happened, but you can't mourn someone forever, can you?

But I had no intention of moving on with Simon, if that was what he was getting at. Only it was hard to tell with him, because he never came out and actually said anything; just vague hints. The whole thing was becoming a bit embarrassing. And it was definitely not something I was keen on repeating. Hence my silent 'Please?' to Mrs Biscuit behind his back.

'But what about my pies?' she asked. 'I'm in the middle of making them.'

'You're always telling me how pastry needs to rest and the filling cool before you add it, which is why I get a soggy bottom,' I reminded her.

Luke sniggered, and Mrs Biscuit let the flour shaker she'd been using fall to the table with a clatter as she took off her apron and wiped her hands. 'Come on then, young master Luke,' she said with an exaggerated sigh. 'We under-lings know our place, don't we? Bring your reading book and we'll have a look at it. So what are Bonkers Ben and Loopy Lucy getting up to this week?'

'That's not their names,' Luke giggled as he followed her out of the room.

10

Mrs Biscuit was silently scolding herself as she took Luke off into the sitting room — but not before she'd taken another couple of almond slices from the cooling rack.

'Are those for us?' Luke asked. 'But Mummy said — '

'That's OK then, I'll have yours.' Mrs Biscuit went to take the plate away, but Luke was too quick for her. She laughed, then put her fingers on her lips and went across to the door, her ear pressed to the wood.

'Miss Doble says it's very rude to listen to other people's conversations,' Luke said.

'And yes, Miss Doble is, of course, absolutely right,' Mrs Biscuit said. 'But the thing is, pet, I'm listening out for the timer on the cooker and not to what they're talking about. I wouldn't dream of doing that.'

Well, not much, she added silently. But she was in a quandary. What was it Simon had to say that was so urgent he had to drive up here to deliver it in person? There was something about that man that made her very uneasy. And talk about bad timing. Just as she was working up to explaining everything to Beth. Now what was she going to do? She was in a right old mess and no mistake. And it was all her own fault. She should have done it sooner and not kept putting it off, waiting for the right moment. If her Norman were still around, God rest his sweet soul, he'd have called her an ostrich. 'Putting your head in the sand, as always,' he'd say. 'One of these days, Ivy, the tide is going to come in, and then where will you be? Much better to face up to things, girl.'

But she hadn't faced up to things, had she? And now it wasn't the tide that was coming in, but a whole blooming tsunami.

She didn't give a hoot if Simon had

overheard what she'd just called him. In fact, 'rasher of wind' was one of her milder descriptions of him, and tempered by the fact that young Luke was in the room. She didn't trust men who were thin, and everything about Simon was thin. Thin, beaky nose; thin hair; long, thin fingers and thin lips. He made Mrs Biscuit shudder. Give her a man with some meat on his bones any day. And as for his sandy eyelashes . . .

Beth said he was cultured and elegant and treated her like a grown-up, if you ever heard anything so plain daft. A grown-up, indeed. Not that it was any of Mrs Biscuit's business, of course. But she'd grown fond of Beth over the months she'd been here, and admired the courageous way she'd faced each hurdle that life had thrown at her. And there had been that many hurdles, the girl should have been a serious contender for the Olympics, the way she'd tackled them all.

But she and Simon, they were wrong for each other. Why couldn't Beth see that? Simon was the most humourless man Mrs Biscuit had ever met, and it grieved her to think of Beth's warmth and sense of fun being slowly frozen out by that cold man, as it surely would be. But the closest she and Beth had ever come to having words was the day Mrs Biscuit had tried to tell her that. Beth's usually warm eyes had gone cold, her mouth set in a thin, tight line.

'I would prefer it if my private life could remain just that, if it's all the same to you,' she'd said curtly. 'And I would also like to remind you that I am an adult and quite capable of making my own mind up about someone. Simon is a good, kind man, and the fact that you and he don't get on is just too bad.'

'Yes, pet, I'm sorry.' Mrs Biscuit was genuine in her apology. 'I shouldn't have said that. You're absolutely right; it's none of my business. My Norman always used to say that I spoke first and thought later. I'm sorry if my bluntness offended you.'

'It didn't,' Beth said gently, the frostiness gone as quickly as it had appeared. 'I'm touched that you worry about me, but you really don't need to, you know. There's nothing serious between me and Simon. We just happen to have the same taste in music and films and go out together occasionally. That's all. Nothing more.'

Mrs Biscuit shook her head now as she and Luke bit into their almond slices. It might be nothing more than the occasional night out as far as Beth was concerned, but she was not sure Simon saw it that way. Still, she shouldn't interfere. Beth was quite right in choking her off about it. She just wished she knew what they were talking about.

11

Simon's thin mouth was pursed in disapproval as he watched Mrs Biscuit and Luke leave. He righted the overturned flour shaker, then took a piece of kitchen paper and dusted his hands carefully.

'I heard what she called me,' he said as he placed the crumpled paper in the already overflowing bin. 'I swear that woman gets more outrageous every day. Why you put up with her, heaven alone knows.'

Because my business would go under without her, I thought, but kept it to myself. I'd long since learnt from experience the futility of trying to persuade either Mrs Biscuit or Simon to see the other's good points. Instead, I murmured: 'She doesn't mean any harm,' although I wasn't entirely convinced that, where Simon was concerned at least, that was entirely true.

'So come on, what's this great news you're bursting to share with me?' I went on, anxious to change the subject and divert his attention from Mrs Biscuit — something not helped by the gales of laughter that were coming from the sitting room. Goodness knew what she and Luke were reading in there, but I doubted it was anything the sainted Miss Doble would approve of.

'Let me guess,' I added, trying to lighten the moment with a feeble attempt at a joke, 'you've found a purple daffodil.'

Simon was an enthusiastic and knowledgeable gardener who collected seeds and cuttings with the single-mindedness of a bird-watcher on the trail of a great crested slubwarbler. He frowned, then looked at me, as he often did when I made a joke, half-bewildered, half-exasperated.

'There's no such thing as a purple daffodil,' he said stiffly. 'My good news is for you, Beth.'

'For me? Well like I said, I could certainly use some, and as I don't do the lottery — '

'My news is better than that.' He relaxed and came towards me, his eyes shining. For a moment I thought he was going to take me in his arms, and stepped back just in case. Instead, he looked around the comfortable chaos of the kitchen and smiled.

'Do you know, Beth, this really is a lovely old house.'

'I like it,' I said carefully, surprised by his abrupt change of subject.

'Do you remember me saying once what a great asset you have here?'

'It's a pity the bank manager doesn't agree with you.' I spoke without thinking as a prickle of unease chased along my spine. Where was he going with this?

'Well, the thing is, I've a client who's seen Brackwith and has fallen in love with it. He's offering really silly money.'

'For Brackwith?' I thought of that

brief moment of despair I'd had during the drive home from Luke's school when I'd wondered if keeping Brackwith was worth all the hassle. But it had only been a fleeting thought, born of weariness. I hadn't really meant it.

'But it's not for sale,' I said crisply. 'I hope you made that clear, Simon.'

'I know, I know. But wait until you hear how much he's offering. It'll blow your mind.'

The sum he mentioned was indeed staggering, but my mind stayed firmly un-blown, and my answer was an emphatic and quite snippy no.

'I hear what you're saying, Beth. But before you give a final answer — '

'I've just given you my final answer. I don't — '

'Just hear me out.' His voice was quiet, persuasive. 'Think about it. You could buy a couple of houses just as good as this and still have money in the bank with what he's offering. It's the offer of a lifetime. You'd be crazy to pass it up. It would solve all your financial problems in one fell swoop.'

'I don't have financial problems. They're sorted.'

'Don't tell me Gerald Hornsby extended your overdraft?'

I stared at him, furious at the way his thin, sandy eyebrows lifted in astonishment. How dare he!

'OK, I won't,' I snapped. 'Because, to be perfectly frank, Simon, my financial situation is none of your damn business. And my problems,' I added, my voice dripping ice, 'if I had any — which I don't — are my concern, not yours.'

Simon pushed a long, thin finger around his shirt collar, which looked as if it had suddenly shrunk. 'Look, it was stupid of me to spring this on you like this. It's come as a shock, I can see that. But all I'm asking, Beth, is that you think about it.'

'There's no point in thinking about it. I won't change my mind.' I turned away, reluctant to let him see how upset I was. How could I explain to him what

Brackwith meant to me? Simon only ever saw houses as bricks, mortar and capital gains. But to me, it was so much more than that. This rambling, shambling old house was going to be the sort of place neither Andrew nor I had known as children: a real home with dogs flopped in front of the kitchen range, muddy boots in the hall and rope swings in the apple trees. I was keeping the dream alive as much for Andrew as for Luke and myself. I owed him that. Because if I hadn't —

'It's one hell of an offer,' Simon persisted.

For once, I was glad of his interruption. It had stopped my thoughts going off down that old familiar path. His narrow face stiffened, a muscle twitching at the corner of his mouth like he was trying really hard not to yell at me.

'As I said, you could buy another place and be mortgage-free.'

'Which part of the word 'no' don't you understand, Simon?' I snapped. 'Because if you think — '

The peal of the front doorbell made us both jump and stopped me saying something I would perhaps have ended up regretting. But then again, perhaps not. I left him in the kitchen and went off to answer the door. The front one wasn't quite as badly warped as the back one, but nevertheless it was impossible to open without a protesting screech.

I'd never have believed I'd ever say this, but I was actually glad to see Joe Tennant standing there. Even if he was staring up in the direction of the rotting window frames with a frown.

'Joe, come along in,' I said, anxious to divert his attention from the windows.

He stopped in the kitchen doorway, a large box in his arms. 'I'm sorry, I didn't realise you had a visitor.'

'No,' I said quickly, and turned to glare at Simon. 'He was just leaving.'

'I'll see myself out,' Simon said. 'Just promise me you'll think about what I said, Beth.'

He was persistent, I'd grant him that. 'Simon, this is Andrew's brother, Joe,' I said as good manners finally caught up with me, even though I was still pretty annoyed with him. 'But of course, you probably know that, don't you? Seeing as you went to school with Andrew.' I turned to Joe. 'Simon says he and Andrew used to be great friends.'

Simon flushed as Joe frowned and said: 'I'm sorry, it was all a long time ago now. Andrew had so many friends.'

'Indeed he did.' Simon glanced at his watch. 'Now, if you'll excuse me, I've got an appointment and I'm already cutting it fine. Nice to meet you, Joe.'

I winced as the front door screeched closed behind him. Joe's eyebrows lifted and I steeled myself for his comment, but he said nothing. My large, comfortable kitchen suddenly seemed to have shrunk as I faced him across the table, which was littered with Mrs Biscuit's half-finished pies.

'I — I'm sorry about this afternoon,' I said quickly, brushing some spilt flour into a tidy pile rather than looking at him. 'In the churchyard. It was — it was a shock. I wasn't expecting to see you there.'

He shrugged. 'No worries. It was my fault. I should have phoned to let you know I was coming. The thing is, Beth — '

'I'll go and get Luke, shall I? He's doing his reading practice with Mrs Biscuit, and I think they'll both be happy for an excuse to stop. I'll just . . . '

I turned and almost ran from the room. Even now, after all these years, I still hadn't worked out what I was going to say to him. 'Sorry' just wasn't going to cut it. I needed more time to work out what to say. Something along the lines of: 'I'm sorry that I didn't pick my words more carefully when I told your brother I was pregnant. I'm sorry I turned my face away from his last goodbye kiss. I'm sorry I got him so mad that he went up a mountain and got himself killed.'

Or words to that effect.

12

At any other time, Joe would have laughed at the speed with which Beth had scurried away, or maybe even been a bit annoyed about it. But at the moment, he was as edgy and nervous as she appeared to be.

He put the box he was carrying on a nearby chair and looked around the crowded kitchen: at the laundry drying above the range, the childish drawings covering the fridge door, the pots of herbs on the windowsill. It was a million miles away from his own streamlined, state-of-the-art kitchen; and yet, for a moment he felt a pang of envy. A pang of sadness, too, as he remembered how this was exactly the sort of kitchen that Andrew always talked about having, when they'd grown up with only the sterile orderliness of a hotel kitchen. In fact, the only thing missing from Andrew's dream kitchen was the dog basket by the side of the cooker. And the dog, of course.

Andrew always favoured cheerful chaos over efficiency, and Joe remembered with painful clarity how excited his brother had been when he'd told him that the kitchen at Brackwith came complete with an old battered but still-working range cooker. Joe felt strangely close to his brother here, much more so than he'd done at the churchyard.

He should have come sooner. It was cowardly of him to have put it off for so long, even though he'd always known his visit would not be welcomed by Beth. Would he have done so if he hadn't come across that old train set of Andrew's? And was now the time to tell Beth the truth about the accident? Would it help her get on with her life?

He sighed. Maybe he should just leave the train set and go. Beth, for one, would be relieved, and it could save them both a lot of awkwardness.

But everything flew out of his head as the kitchen door opened and Luke stood there. The breath caught in Joe's throat at the sight of him. It was like putting the clock back and seeing a young Andrew staring up at him: the same stick-thin arms and legs, the same piercing blue eyes and steady gaze. The only difference was that Luke had inherited his mother's vivid red curls. Seeing the boy took Joe right back to those early years when he and Andrew were children and once again, and a deep sadness swept over him at the loss of his younger brother; a sadness that had never gone away even though, for most of the time at least, he managed to push it to the back of his mind.

Unlike the guilt. That never went away.

And now, with Andrew's son staring up at him, that guilt became almost unbearable.

'Hello, Luke,' he said, cursing himself as his voice came out strained and nervous. He'd seen pictures of the boy, of course; Beth had been very good about sending a regular supply to him every Christmas and birthday. But none of them had prepared him for this. 'I'm — I'm your Uncle Joe.'

'I know. Mummy says I have to say thank-you for all the presents, even though I've already done it.' He flashed his mother an indignant look. 'I liked the Lego fire station best of all. It was awesome.'

'I said it would be nice if you said thank-you in person,' Beth said quietly.

'What person?' Luke looked mystified and Joe laughed. As he did so, the tension inside him began to uncoil.

'I'm glad you liked it, Luke,' he said, and made a mental note to thank his PA for telling him the kind of presents a six-year-old boy would like. The fire station had, it appeared, been a hit.

'Would you like to see it?' Luke said. 'It's in my room. It took Mummy hours and hours to make it — and she got very cross while she was doing it, and had to take it all apart and start again because she'd gone wrong right at the beginning. Even though I *told* her it was wrong. And she said a rude word which Miss Doble — that's my teacher — said we must never, ever say.'

'Luke, please,' Beth protested, her face scarlet. 'Uncle Joe doesn't want to hear that.'

'But it's true, Mummy. You said that it was — '

'I know what I said. I also said you weren't to repeat it.'

'Then you said I have to be very careful how I play with it, because you're never ever going to make it again. But I've only broken it twice, and then only a little bit, which I could fix myself.'

'Oh dear.' Joe's lips twitched as he turned to Beth, whose face was still scarlet. 'I'm sorry my present caused you such problems. I'll have to think of something different next time.'

'No, it's all right,' Luke assured him. 'I'm getting really good at building with Lego. Much better than Mummy, so

110

it'll be all right to buy me more.'

'Luke,' Beth said sharply. Joe had forgotten how readily Beth blushed and took pity on her.

'I'm very glad to hear that,' he said quickly. 'But today I've brought something else I think you might like, Luke. It's a train set that used to belong to your daddy when he was about the age you are now.'

'A train set? For me to keep?'

'For you to keep.'

'Is it in that box?'

Joe nodded and handed him the box. 'It is.'

'Oh, wow. That's really totally cool. Daniel Masters has got a train set. I bet it's better than his. Does it have lots of track?'

Joe nodded. 'And an engine shed. And some points. And a tunnel.'

'Look, Luke, why don't you and Uncle Joe go into the sitting room so Mrs Biscuit and I can get on with dinner?' Beth suggested. 'Mr Lawrence is going out early this evening and she's promised him steak and kidney pie.'

'But I thought we were having chicken and bacon pie,' Luke said. 'It's my favourite.'

'She's spoiling you and making a chicken and bacon pie just for you,' Beth said. 'But only if you've finished your reading practice. You have, haven't you?'

Luke nodded. 'Would you like to stay and have some of my pie, Uncle Joe?' Luke asked. 'Mrs Biscuit's pies are awesome.'

'Well, I hadn't planned — ' he began, but stopped as Beth began to speak at the same time.

'Luke, your uncle probably needs to get back,' Beth said, then added quickly, 'But, of course, if you'd like to join us, we'll eat in about an hour, and you'd be very welcome. Mrs Biscuit always makes enough to feed an army.'

Joe felt himself torn. One part of him wanted to get as far away as possible. But the other wanted to spend a little more time with the boy who reminded him so much of his younger brother. And then there was the added temptation of Mrs Biscuit's 'awesome' pies. It was almost too much to resist.

'Well, if you're sure — ' he began.

'Yeah, right!' Luke yelled, and dragged him towards the sitting room. 'Shall I clear a space on the floor? How much room does it take up? Do you have sidings and a station? Daniel has a level crossing . . . '

Joe laughed as he allowed himself to be led into the sitting room. He'd only stay for an hour or two, then maybe he could have that quiet word with Beth after dinner when Luke was in bed.

If his nerve held out.

13

I left Luke and Joe on their hands and knees in the middle of the sitting room, the chairs pushed back against the wall to give them as much space as possible. Luke was chattering away like an over-excited magpie as they unpacked the box. I didn't mean to invite Joe to stay for dinner, but the look on his face when he saw Luke had touched me deeply. I knew he felt as I did every time I looked into Luke's face and saw Andrew's eyes laughing back at me. For the first time, I felt myself softening slightly towards Andrew's stern older brother.

I went back into the kitchen, where Mrs Biscuit was busy putting the finishing touches on the pies. 'I'm afraid there's going to be one extra for dinner,' I said. 'Luke invited Joe to stay.'

Mrs Biscuit looked up, her face

flushed from the pie she'd just taken out of the oven. 'Joe?'

'Yes, I'm sorry. Nobody was more surprised than I was when he accepted, although Luke gave him little choice. I must say, when he first got here, he looked like he couldn't get away fast enough. But now I've left them in the sitting room playing trains, and it looks like they could be some time.' I paused and looked more closely at Mrs Biscuit. 'Are you all right? You're looking a bit — '

'It's hot in here,' she said quickly. 'Either that, or it's my age.'

'I'm sorry,' I went on, puzzled by her unusual evasiveness. 'Look, I hope this hasn't inconvenienced you. I really should've checked with you first. That is all right, isn't it?'

Mrs Biscuit's face went a deeper shade of crimson. 'Well, yes, of course it's all right. It's just . . . well, I've made arrangements. I — I'm going out. To the concert. With Mr Lawrence.'

I was relieved to have discovered the

cause of her obvious unease. Mr Lawrence had asked her out on several occasions but she'd always made an excuse not to go, until now. I couldn't help teasing her just a little. 'But I thought you said you weren't going — that choral music isn't your thing?'

'It still isn't. Give me Daniel O'Donnell any day,' she said briskly as she placed cutlery on a tray. 'But I just felt like a change, that's all. It's no big deal, so don't you go reading anything into it, OK?'

'OK,' I said with a grin.

'I'll just go and take Mr Lawrence's supper in to him, then I'll be off and get ready. Now I've put the timer on. The other pies are going to need another twenty minutes, if you'll listen out for it.'

I was still smiling as Mrs Biscuit bustled out, her round face still flushed. She was obviously looking forward to going out with Mr Lawrence after all, which the old man would be delighted about.

I could hear the murmur of voices from the guests' dining room, where Mr Lawrence was having his early supper. From the other side of the hall came Luke's excited chatter as the railway began to take shape. I sat down in the easy chair by the range and allowed myself a rare moment of peace in what had been a full-on, hectic day. I should have used the quiet time to think about what I was going to say to Joe. Instead, I made myself a cup of tea, and was partway through one of Mrs Biscuit's almond slices when the kitchen door crashed open.

Mrs Biscuit stood in the doorway, her face the colour of putty, her eyes wild with terror. 'Mr Lawrence!' she cried. 'He's been poisoned! It's happening again. Oh, dear God, it's happening again. Please help him. Get an ambulance. Tell them to hurry. He's dying.'

14

Luke didn't understand the seriousness of Mr Lawrence's collapse. As far as he was concerned, it was the most exciting thing to happen since a rook fell down the sitting room chimney and went on a sooty rampage around the house. He bounded upstairs to watch the ambulance for as long as he could from his bedroom window.

'Do you think it was a heart attack?' I asked Joe, hugely relieved that Mr Lawrence was conscious, though breathing with difficulty, and on his way to hospital. 'The paramedics weren't very forthcoming, were they?'

'They'll know more when he gets there,' Joe said.

Mrs Biscuit had insisted on following the ambulance to the hospital. 'His only daughter lives in Australia, so he's all on his own,' she'd said. 'He'll want to see a familiar face.'

'It was such a shock,' I said. 'When I came in and saw him there, I thought — I thought . . . ' I shivered and wrapped my arms around my body. Seeing him like that had taken me straight back to the evening my father collapsed and died. I was eleven years old and had just started at secondary school. Dad and I had been on our own — my mother was working late, as always — and I was chattering away to him about my day, when he'd suddenly given a little cry and slumped forward. Poor Mr Lawrence's collapse had brought the paralysing shock, the utter helplessness and panic sharply back, and I couldn't shake them off.

'He's in the best place,' Joe said. 'Beth, are you OK?'

'I'm fine. Look, I think I'll go and clear up in the dining room.' I needed to be doing something — anything — to chase away that image. 'I never thought I'd say this, but I'm really glad we haven't got any other guests staying at the moment. If it had happened this time last week, the dining room would have been full. Which would have been traumatic for everyone.'

'Is business not so good then?' Joe asked as he followed me into the dining room.

'No, no, it's good,' I said hastily. 'But we've deliberately not taken bookings this week because we thought we were having the builders in.'

'And now you're not?'

'I'll just go and get a tray from the kitchen. If you could start by picking up the broken glass, that'll be great. But be careful though, won't you?'

My trip to the kitchen would, I hope, give me the chance to avoid answering that particular question which, now I came to think of it, was none of his damn business! How dare he take advantage of my momentary wobble to quiz me about the state of my business. The little spurt of anger chased away the dark shadows as I regained my control.

'Why do you think Mrs Biscuit said he'd been poisoned?' I asked him when I returned. 'That it was happening again? What was happening again?'

He shrugged as we loaded a tray with the sorry remains of Mrs Biscuit's lovely pie and the broken crockery and glass. 'I have no idea. One of those things people say in a panic, I guess.'

'I suppose so. It was so unlike her, though. Me, I worry and flap about everything from the economic down-turn to which day to put the dustbin out. But she's always struck me as a calm, level-headed person. Nothing fazes her.'

'Finding someone face down in your steak and kidney pie would phase most people, I imagine,' Joe said.

And perhaps, like me, she had a painful memory. I remembered that she was a widow, though she was not very forthcoming about her past. She just muttered something about 'water under the bridge' when I asked, and I'd assumed that it wasn't something she wanted to talk about, so had never pushed her. Maybe her husband had died suddenly, like Dad; and once again the memory of my terrified eleven-year-old self resurfaced. My hands shook slightly as I picked up the last of the cutlery and bundled up the soiled tablecloth ready for the washing machine.

'It was very kind of you to offer to drive her to the hospital,' I said to Joe. 'I was surprised when she refused. She looked in no fit state.'

'I suspect she's one of those people who feel better when they're doing something.' He picked up the tray and followed me into the kitchen with it. 'Look, Beth, I shouldn't worry too much about Mrs — what did you call her?'

'Mrs Biscuit. It's Luke's name for her. Her real name is Mrs Biston, but the name has sort of stuck.'

He gave a small smile. 'It suits her. She's one of life's copers, you'll see.'

I bent down to put the tablecloth in the washing machine and, as I stood up, everything went misty. My head began to swim and I grasped the edge of the table for support.

'Are you OK?' He was at my side in an instant. He put his arms around me and I let go of the table and sagged against him. Through the cool crispness of his shirt I could feel the hardness of his chest; hear the steady thud of his heartbeat. I put my hand flat against his chest and let it rest there. Just for one mad moment, I felt safe and protected, and wanted that feeling to go on forever. It was so long since I'd felt a pair of strong arms around me; smelt the fresh tang of a man's aftershave. If my knees had felt weak before, now they felt like they'd suddenly turned to custard. And my head to cotton wool.

What, oh what had I been thinking of? I pulled away, embarrassed, hoping he hadn't noticed my moment of utter madness. 'I'm fine,' I muttered. 'Just felt a bit woolly for a moment.' Woolly? That was one way of putting it. Plain, stark raving bonkers would be another.

'Here, sit down for a minute.' He pulled out a chair and led me to it. 'It'll be a touch of delayed shock, I expect.'

'Yes, that'll be it,' I said shakily.

'Can I get you a cup of tea?' he asked. 'Or something stronger?'

'No, thanks. I'll be fine in a moment. I'm not usually this wimpish.'

'It's not being wimpish at all,' he said. 'You've had a shock. It's natural to be affected by it.'

At that moment, Luke burst into the room. 'Mummy, do you know where my fire engine is?' he said. 'I can't find it anywhere.'

Joe stood up. 'I'll help you find it. But how about you and I put the train set away first, while Mummy sits here quietly for a few minutes?'

I was indeed grateful for those few minutes, and by the time he came back I had regained both my equilibrium and my sanity.

'The fire engine was in the bathroom, and now he's gone upstairs to fetch his ambulance,' Joe told me. 'We've packed the train set away.'

I smiled. 'Thank you. But if I know my son, you would've done most of the packing away while he supervised.'

'Just like his father,' he said with a nod. 'Are you feeling better now?'

'Thanks, much better. It's just that I haven't eaten very much today, and it's caught up with me. You're still staying for supper, aren't you?'

He glanced at his watch. 'It's getting late.'

'Please don't go.' The words shot out of my mouth before I could stop them. I might have recovered my equilibrium, but I wasn't sure how long Mrs Biscuit would be at the hospital, and I didn't want to be on my own. And if the price I had to pay for company meant that we'd have to talk about Andrew's accident, then so be it. It was about time we cleared the air. I couldn't keep putting it off.

'You promised Luke you'd stay,' I said. 'In fact, you're welcome to stay the night. We've plenty of room, as I said. We have no other guests, so you can take your pick. Apart from Room Three. We . . . we've had a problem with the roof.'

'That's what the builders were supposed to fix, were they?' he asked.

'They've . . . got another job on somewhere,' I said, which wasn't a complete lie. When I'd phoned them to say I was going to have to put them off for a while, they were very understanding and said not to worry, that they had so much work on at the moment, it was coming out of their ears. But I figured Joe didn't need to know that I was the one who had changed the arrangements, not them.

'So, would you like to stay? That valley road can be a nightmare in the dark. And it sounds like it's started to rain.'

He peered out of the kitchen window into inky blackness. For a moment I thought he was going to refuse. But he surprised me by saying: 'Thanks. I must admit the thought of the valley road in the dark and wet isn't appealing, particularly as it's a few years since I've done it. So I'll take you up on your offer, if that's OK. But you must let me pay the going rate.'

'Indeed you will not,' I said sharply. I didn't like Joe. Well, it's hard to like someone who has called you a spoilt, selfish brat, isn't it? Added to which, he was cold, hard and judgemental, and made little effort to hide his disapproval of me and my life choices. As for what happened just now when I'd stumbled, well, I'd overreacted. It was the shock of Mr Lawrence, then thinking about Dad, all combined with lack of food — and, of course, Mr Horseface. No wonder I'd had a 'moment'. But I was over it now. No danger of another one.

But I'd seen a different side of him when he was with Luke and the two of them had really hit it off. And I hadn't been exaggerating when I'd said I didn't know how Mrs Biscuit and I would have coped with Mr Lawrence if he hadn't been there.

As for him paying to stay here, it was out of the question. When Andrew and I had overstretched ourselves financially to scrape up the deposit to buy Brackwith, Joe had helped us out on several occasions. In fact, one of the many things Andrew and I had rowed about in our short and often stormy marriage was the way he'd go to his brother for money if things got tight, instead of pulling our belts in and sorting things out for ourselves.

'After everything you did for us,' I said, 'clearing the overdraft and — '

'Damn him.' Joe scowled. 'He'd no right to tell you.'

'He had every right,' I snapped, back on the defensive again. 'He was my husband. We had no secrets from each other.'

'What?' He looked confused for a moment, then he rubbed his hand across his eyes. 'I'm sorry, Beth. I'm talking nonsense. Just ignore me. Like you, I've had a long day.'

I meant to smile and say no worries,

that I was pretty fluent in nonsense-speak myself. But as often happens when I'm stressed, my brain and mouth aren't always in sync with each other. Something entirely different came out. 'I'm sorry I was rude to you in the churchyard, Joe. It was the shock of seeing you like that. I — I wasn't expecting . . . '

'Forget it.' His voice was clipped. 'I have.'

'I don't know what we'd have done if you hadn't been here this evening,' I went on. 'First aid's not really my thing.'

'I remember. Andrew's finger,' Joe said, his usually sombre face softened by a smile. He was referring to a time when Andrew had been showing me the way 'proper chefs' chop onions but had sliced the top off his finger instead. Joe'd been with us that day and, while I was flapping around like a hen on hurry-up pills, he'd quietly and calmly dealt with it.

'If I remember correctly,' he continued, 'you spent the entire time trying and failing to open the completely inadequate first-aid tin you had at the time.'

'That's not fair,' I protested, joining in with his laughter as we shared the memory. 'You were in the Mountain Rescue team at the time. Of course your first-aid skills were better than mine, though mine have improved — along with the contents of the first-aid tin — since Luke took up skateboarding. They've had to, with the amount of skin he manages to scrape off every time he goes out on the wretched thing. So do you still belong to Mountain Rescue?'

I spoke without thinking and could have bitten my tongue. Joe's smile faded and his mouth tightened as he shook his head. How stupid was I? It was Joe's teammates who'd stretchered him and Andrew down the day of the accident.

'Not anymore,' he said. 'My fitness isn't up to scratch.'

'I'm sorry. I should have thought.' I

remembered the wheelchair at the funeral. 'Is it your leg?'

He nodded curtly. 'More pins than my old granny's pin cushion.'

'That's tough.' There was a little awkward silence. Then I went on: 'You will stay, Joe, won't you? It'll take me less than five minutes to get the room ready. Maybe you'd like to read Luke his bedtime story while I do it? He'd love that. And, of course, we've got one of Mrs Biscuit's steak and kidney pies for dinner. Guaranteed awesome.'

'Then how can I refuse?' He smiled.

I was glad he had accepted. Half an hour later, as I was putting the pie in the oven to warm through, the phone rang.

15

Joe shook his head as Beth hurried out in to the hall to answer the phone. What sort of an idiot was he, for pity's sake? Why didn't he just go while he had the chance? He'd done what he'd come to do. He'd checked out the place for himself. And the information he'd had was right. The house was, indeed, in a sorry state once you looked past the fresh flowers and new paint. And it sounded as if Beth's finances were stretched to the limit. He wouldn't mind betting she'd put the builders off, not the other way around.

She'd really given the place her best shot, he'd grant her that. On the surface at least, the place looked very well kept and together. It was only when you looked closer that you could see the problems.

He looked around the kitchen. She'd

made little structural change to the room since she and Andrew had bought the place from the farmer's widow. They'd inherited a rusty old kitchen range, a large deal table with wonky legs that had seen better days, and a dusty oak dresser that covered the length of one wall. Now the range was polished out of all recognition and filled the room with its cosy warmth. The dresser had had a similar transformation and was obviously lovingly cared for. The cheerful plates and sparkling glassware that ranged along its shelves were reflected in the soft sheen of its well-polished surface. At least, the bits of the surface you could see. Most of it was littered with childish drawings, haphazard piles of papers and some Lego bricks heaped in a blue pottery bowl. As for the table, Joe gave it a gentle push and was relieved to see it stood firm and sturdy in the middle of the flagstone floor. It was covered by a blue and white checked oil cloth and already laid up for supper.

Joe was impressed in spite of himself. He could imagine guests being charmed by the ambience of this homely room. Beth had obviously worked hard to make it, and probably the rest of the house, warm and welcoming. There was no doubt it was a comfortable home as well as a business. He could see that, given time and a whole heap of money, she could well have a successful enterprise here. But she was seriously under-financed, and that was no way to run a business, he thought with a sad shake of his head. He'd be doing her no favours if he didn't warn her of the dangers of throwing good money after bad. Guests were much more demanding these days, as he knew full well, and wanted more than cosy kitchens and a hearty breakfast.

That was one of the things he'd come here to tell her, only now probably wasn't the right time. He thought back to what it had felt like when she'd stumbled in the kitchen and he'd put his arms around her to support her.

She'd felt like thistledown in his arms; like a puff of wind would blow her over. She'd obviously been shaken rigid by the old man's collapse. She'd tried to hold it together for the sake of the boy, and Joe admired her for that; but he could see the effort it had cost her, and he wondered if it brought back the trauma of Andrew's death, which would explain the haunted look in her eyes.

But she was still as spiky as ever, he thought as he picked up the brightly coloured pieces of Lego and began fitting them together. He was right to be cautious. He'd nearly blown it by flaring up when she'd been talking about him helping out with the mortgage. If she thought he knew about the visit to the bank manager, she'd have been even more annoyed, and probably thrown him out there and then.

'Shall we play ambulances now, Uncle Joe?' Luke asked as he charged into the room, fire engine in one hand, ambulance in the other. He knelt down on the floor and began pushing the toys around. 'Would you like the ambulance or the fire engine?'

Joe shook his head. The last time he'd knelt down, back in the churchyard earlier this afternoon, he'd had problems getting up again. That was something he was in no hurry to repeat.

'How about I make up this Lego for you?' he said. 'What was it?'

Luke frowned. 'It was a helicopter, but it had a crash landing, and Mummy says she's not going to put it together again. And I've lost the nistructions. Can you do it without nistructions?'

'I can try.' It had been a long time since Joe had handled Lego but thought he could probably still puzzle it out, with or without 'nistructions'. 'OK, you find me all the long grey pieces, and I'll start on the body.' Luke soon became absorbed in shifting through the bricks.

'So, how's school?' Joe asked. 'What do you like best?'

'Play time.'

Joe grinned. He was, indeed, his

father's son. 'Nothing else?'

'Lunch time as well. Although that isn't as nice as the food Mrs Biscuit makes. And Melissa Stanley was sick yesterday. All over her shoes.'

'Oh dear.' Joe decided against following up that particular topic of conversation. 'What about reading? Do you like that?'

Luke shrugged. 'Sometimes, if the words aren't too hard. And I like the funny stories. There's one about a dancing dog. That's my favourite.'

'Is it this one?' Joe reached across and picked up the reading book that was on a nearby chair, next to a red bag with the name of the school printed on it in bold black letters. As he bent down to put the book back, he noticed a piece of yellow paper that had fallen to the floor. He stretched down and picked it up. It was a parental consent form.

'A trip to Coniston, eh?' He smiled. 'That sounds a lot of fun.'

Luke nodded. 'But I nearly didn't get to go. Mummy forgot to put the form in my bag. And Miss Doble said, 'Oh,

Luke, not again.' Mummy often forgets things.'

Joe looked down at the paper and saw, printed across the top, 'To be returned by the 15th at the latest!!!' It had been underlined three times in thick red ink. He checked the date on his watch. Today was the 16th. Tricky.

Would the trip to Coniston include a hike up the Old Man? he wondered. Probably not. He wouldn't fancy taking a group of six-year-olds up a mountain like that, which could be quite challenging in places. But then again, Andrew hadn't been much older than Luke was now when he'd finally managed to wear Joe down. He'd been on at him for ages to take him fell walking, promising that he could keep up. Their parents didn't care where the boys went as long as they were out of the way. So after that first outing when Andrew, true to his word, had indeed kept up, the pair of them had spent all their spare time exploring the fells and mountains in the area, Andrew getting more and more ambitious each time. As he got older and the routes became more challenging, he'd shown himself to be a natural climber. He'd loved the challenge of the mountains, particularly Brackwith Pike. It was small wonder he'd been so keen to buy a house in its shadow.

'Did my daddy climb up Coniston?' Luke asked as he handed Joe a neat stack of grey bricks.

'Lots of times,' Joe said. 'The Old Man was one of his favourite mountains.'

'The Old Man?' Luke giggled. 'That's a funny name. Why is it called that?'

Joe shrugged. 'I'm not sure. Maybe from a certain angle it looks like a giant man lying down.'

'I'd like to go climbing,' Luke said suddenly. 'Do you think Miss Doble will let us climb the Old Man?'

'I think it's very, very unlikely,' Joe said with absolute certainty.

'Then will you take me?'

Joe's hands stilled. If Andrew was still

around, he'd have bought Luke his first pair of climbing boots by now, that was for sure. Should he offer to do so? Better check with Beth first.

As for himself, did he miss the mountains? He'd thought not. He had managed to keep it to the back of his mind, even when driving up here earlier this afternoon when he was more concerned about what he was going to say to Beth. But now, being here, so close to one of his favourite climbs, he felt a pang of regret to think that he'd never again climb that tricky traverse up to the summit, from where you could look down on the valley and across to the Helvellyn range in the distance. Never again breathe in lungfuls of the freshest, sweetest air in the whole world.

Maybe it would have been better if he hadn't come back, after all. Maybe he should have sent someone else to see Beth; someone who wasn't so emotionally involved with the place. He fixed the rotor blades on the reassembled helicopter and handed it to Luke, unwilling to answer his question, which was thankfully now forgotten in the pleasure of having the helicopter back in one piece.

'Look, why don't I put this in here, ready for school tomorrow?' Joe said as he put the form in Luke's bag.

'Will you be here tomorrow?' Luke asked. 'I can show you my skateboard if you like. I haven't had it very long so I keep falling off a lot. But I don't hurt myself because I've got knee pads and a helmet.'

'Good idea,' Joe said. 'But I'm afraid I can't stay. I've got to get back to London tomorrow.' He felt a pang of genuine regret at the thought of having to go back, and wished he could have stayed longer. But Kate would never forgive him if he missed her big night. The law firm where she worked was putting on a big bash for some of its major clients and this was her chance to shine. He found that sort of thing a terrible bore, but he'd promised to be there to offer her some moral support.

A pity though. He'd have loved to have spent more time with Luke. But perhaps now the ice had broken, he could see him more often. That would be infinitely easier if he could only prise Beth away from this money pit of a house, and make her see that the best thing she could do for herself and Luke would be to sell the place. He'd have to pick his moment though, judging from the way she'd flown at him earlier. Maybe after dinner when they'd relaxed a bit after 'Mrs Biscuit's awesome pie', he'd be able to broach the subject.

At that moment Beth came back into the kitchen. He could see in an instant that something was badly wrong. Her face was grey, her eyes wide.

'Is everything OK?' he asked.

She shook her head. 'Th — that was Mrs. Biscuit on the phone,' she said. 'I could hardly make out what she was saying, she was in such a state.'

'Mr Lawrence? Is he — ?'

'No, no, he's hanging in there,

although still very poorly. But — but she said . . . ' She put her hand to her mouth and swayed slightly.

'Here, sit down.' For the second time that evening, Joe led her towards a chair. 'Take your time.'

'I — I still can't believe it,' she said, her voice barely above a whisper so that Joe had to strain to hear it. 'I think she said not to eat the pies. That they might — that they might be poisoned.'

16

'What's wrong, Mummy?' Luke asked uneasily. 'You look funny.'

I tried to pull myself together for his sake. He was looking across the table at me, his small face puckered with anxiety.

'I'm just a bit worried about poor Mr Lawrence, that's all,' I said gently.

'Is he coming home from hospital?' he asked.

'Not yet. He's still quite poorly. I've just spoken to Mrs Biscuit on the phone.' I almost succeeded in making my voice sound normal. 'They — they think Mr Lawrence may have eaten something that upset his tummy.'

'Like when I ate all those plums?' Luke asked.

'Exactly like that,' I said, wishing with all my heart it turned out to be something that simple. All this talk about poisoning was freaking me out.

'Is she still at the hospital?' Joe asked.

'I'm not sure.' I frowned as I tried to recall exactly what she had said. It had been difficult to pick it out. 'She sounded in a really bad way. She wasn't making much sense; I could hardly make out what she was saying, except 'don't eat the pies'. Then she kept going on about how it was happening again, like she did earlier. But when I asked her what she meant by that, she didn't answer. I couldn't get her calm enough to tell me. What do you think she meant?'

Joe frowned. 'Who knows? The poor woman's in shock, I guess.'

'I know what you're going to say. You're going to ask me what I know about her, aren't you?' I could feel my face burning as I thought of the many times Simon had asked that very same question. But Joe just shrugged.

'Well, she turned up here a few months ago as a guest,' I said. 'She was booked in for the week. But she was so horrified by the breakfast I served her that she stayed on, and has been cooking for me ever since. She said she hated retirement and that it was good to be needed again. And boy did I need her. Andrew used to say I was the only person he knew who could ruin beans on toast.'

'I remember,' Joe said, and I'd forgotten how his eyes used to soften when he laughed, making him look ten years younger. I hadn't seen him laugh in what seemed forever. But when I first knew him, he and Andrew used to laugh a lot. They were such good friends back then, not just brothers.

Poor Joe. I hadn't given much thought to how much he must miss Andrew. Grief can be a very selfish emotion. You tend to forget that other people are grieving too. Time, I reckoned, to clear the air between us.

I took a deep breath and went for it. 'Joe . . . that day of the accident — '

'How about we keep this conversation for another time?' he said with a warning glance across at Luke who, although appearing to be totally engrossed in lining up his toys in front of the range, would, I knew from experience, be listening to our every word, ready to repeat them back at me at the most awkward moment. I flushed, embarrassed that Joe had to remind me of that fact. Talk about Bad Mother of the Year. What had I been thinking of? Miss Doble was right about me, that's for sure.

'Mrs Biscuit will be coming back, won't she?' Luke asked when, as if on cue, he looked up from his toys, his eyes anxious as he scanned our faces.

'Of course she will, sweetheart,' I hurried to reassure him. 'Just as soon as Mr Lawrence is feeling a bit better.'

'Mrs Biscuit's the best cook in the whole wide world,' he told Joe. 'And she tells wicked stories. And she says Simon's a bad smell who — '

'Luke, why don't you go and wash your hands before dinner?' I cut in before he could get any further. 'It's chicken and bacon pie, remember?'

'Chicken and bacon pie, yay!' He

punched the air as he stood up.

I must have misheard what Mrs Biscuit had said. There was no way it could have been the pie that caused Mr Lawrence's collapse. But as I went to put it in the oven, Joe took it from me and placed it on the kitchen windowsill.

'I think it might be better if we had something else,' he said. 'Do you have any eggs?'

'For pity's sake, you can't possibly think . . . ' I began, then stopped. It was one thing to risk myself to prove I trusted Mrs Biscuit — but to risk Luke?

'I do a mean omelette,' Joe said. 'Would you like one, Luke?' he asked as Luke came back into the room. From the time he'd taken, he'd obviously done no more than wave his hands in the direction of the tap.

Joe had just finished cooking the omelettes when the kitchen door opened and Mrs Biscuit came in, her face the colour of cold porridge. The poor soul looked as if she'd aged ten years in the last few hours.

'Is — is it all right if I come back here? Only, I had to tell the hospital where I'd be, in case . . . ' Her voice trailed away. The room crackled with the tension of those unspoken words left hanging in the air.

'Of course,' I said, a forced brightness in my voice. 'Why would you not? If you remember, we said that tomorrow we'd get on with some of the advanced preparations for that party of ten booked in next week. Who's going to cook them if you're not here? Me?'

For Luke's sake, she attempted a wobbly smile. 'That looks good.' She pointed to the omelette.

'Joe made it,' Luke said between mouthfuls. 'It's awesome.'

'Want some?' Joe asked. 'I can soon knock you up one.'

She shook her head. 'No thanks, Joe.' Her voice cracked with weariness. 'I couldn't eat a thing.'

It was weird hearing her call Joe by his Christian name. Usually she had a rigid rule about what she called 'over-familiarity'. It took me forever to persuade her to call me Beth. But then, it had been one of those days when nothing was normal.

'Look, Joe made this helicopter for me without any nistructions.' Luke showed her the helicopter that was parked up next to his plate. 'He's a much better Lego builder than Mummy.'

He prattled away at her as she sat down at the table opposite him. She wasn't really listening but staring straight ahead, her face still the colour of porridge, her hands shaking. It worried me to think she'd done the forty-minute drive from the hospital in that state. I went to the drinks cupboard and poured her a stiff measure of brandy.

'Here, drink this.' I placed the glass of amber-coloured liquid on the table in front of her.

She drew back as if the glass contained arsenic. 'No, thank you. I never touch the stuff.'

'Well, there's sherry, if you prefer,' I said. 'It'll make you feel — '

'For heaven's sake,' she snapped, 'weren't you listening? Didn't I just say I don't touch the stuff?'

There was a sudden shocked silence. Luke looked as startled by her harsh voice as I was. It was as if the dear old family labrador had suddenly morphed into a rottweiler with a raging toothache.

Joe cleared his throat and touched her gently on the shoulder. 'You look all in,' he said quietly to her. 'Why don't you take yourself off to bed?'

'I will.' She turned to me, her small currant eyes swimming with tears. 'I'm so sorry,' she whispered. 'I don't know what came over me. Please forgive me.'

'Nothing to forgive,' I hurried to reassure her. 'Joe's right, you look done in. Go on to bed.'

She nodded, then looked across at the windowsill and pointed to the two pies sitting there. 'Thank God I was in time. You didn't eat them, then.' No rottweiler now. Instead she looked like someone who'd gone ten rounds with a heavyweight boxer and was still reeling from it. 'They — the hospital said they'll be making a report. Environmental Health, Police. Whatever. I don't know. I couldn't quite take it all in. But they were very insistent. Said it was important not to throw anything away. So what happened to the pie Mr Lawrence was eating? They'll want that as well, I'm sure.'

'It's in the bin. But let's not worry about that now, eh?' I said soothingly. 'It'll all still be here in the morning.'

Her shoulders slumped, and as I put my arm around her I could feel she was trembling. 'Do you want some cocoa or anything?' I asked, but she shook her head. 'Then go on up now. And don't you dare do breakfast in the morning. I'll do it.'

Her face crumpled. 'I'm so sorry I shouted at you, Beth,' she said, then turned to Luke with a brave attempt at normality. 'What an old grump I am. See what happens when you don't eat broccoli, young Luke. But don't you worry, I'll be better in the morning.'

'Then you'll have some broccoli?' Luke asked gravely, his eyes wide.

'Triple helpings, I promise.'

Joe's omelettes could have been made from sawdust and toenail clippings for all the pleasure either of us got from eating them. Only Luke ate with his customary conviction that the food was about to run out and this could be his last meal for days. As Joe and I pushed food around our plates, Luke prattled happily on, his conversation peppered as usual with the thoughts and sayings of Miss Doble, and what would happen if he went into school again tomorrow without the Coniston form.

'Luke,' I protested, 'I'm sure Uncle Joe doesn't want to hear that.' As always, just thinking about Luke's teacher made me come over all inadequate. Miss Wonder Woman Doble wouldn't have flailed around like I did. She'd have taken complete control, resuscitated Mr Lawrence, cooked a three-course gourmet meal — and all,

153

no doubt, while singing all eight verses of 'Abide With Me'.

'Anyway, young man, it's way past your bedtime,' I said. 'Come along.'

'Can Uncle Joe read me my bedtime story?'

'I'm sure he won't want to — ' I began. But Joe cut across.

'I'd love to,' he said. 'What do you want me to read?'

'Something short,' I said quickly. 'Otherwise he'll have you there all night.'

When he came back down, I was able to ask the question that had been gnawing away at me ever since Mrs Biscuit had come back. 'What do you think it all means, Joe? Mrs Biscuit said something about the police. You don't think — they surely don't think . . . '

'I don't think anything,' he said firmly. 'And neither should you. Let's face that tomorrow, shall we?'

There was some measure of comfort in the fact that he'd used the word 'we'. 'You're welcome to stay another night,'

I said. 'Well, stay as long as you like.' I found myself mentally crossing my fingers. What was wrong with me? Earlier today I couldn't get away from him fast enough. But now I had no idea what tomorrow would hold, and hoped it was just the effects of shock that had Mrs Biscuit talking of poisoning and investigations by the Environmental Health people, and maybe even the police being involved. If that story got around, my business would be dead in the water. It seemed very selfish of me to be fretting over that while poor Mr Lawrence was so unwell, but I couldn't help it.

'I'd planned on going back tomorrow,' Joe said. 'But if you'd like me to stay, I'd just need to make a few phone calls.'

'No, no, that's fine,' I said, backtracking hastily as I cursed myself for my moment of weakness. 'Please don't change any arrangements on my account. I know how busy you are.'

My voice must have come out more

sharply than I'd intended, because he looked at me steadily for a moment and then stood up. 'Look, I'm sorry,' he said. 'It's been quite a day. I think I'll get to bed, if that's OK.'

It wasn't until I dragged myself off to bed and realised I was still wearing my bank-manager-visiting suit that I remembered I hadn't phoned my mother. She'd been 'at a meeting' according to Sally, her PA, when I'd called earlier; and although Sally had offered to take a message, I'd declined. And then again, I didn't think 'Hi, thanks for getting the bank manager off my back, even though you'd said you wouldn't' was hardly the sort of message to leave on her voice-mail.

Forgetting to say thank-you? Another black mark from Miss Doble to go with the one I'd already earned that day for failing to get the parental consent form back on the due day. What would be next?

17

Joe closed the bedroom door quietly and looked around him, nodding approvingly at what he saw. Like the rest of the house, the ambience was warm, welcoming and spotlessly clean. The peach-coloured walls were calming, and the vintage oak furniture gleamed as the scent of beeswax polish and lavender hung soft in the air. Beth certainly had the touch when it came to interior design. Who needed fancy spa baths and polished marble when you could have this? Maybe he should offer her a job. What, he wondered as a matter of interest, would she have made of the hotel he'd recently acquired near Stratford?

He sat down on the bed, with its crisp white bed linen and deep, fluffy pillows, tempted to curl up in it there and then; he hadn't been exaggerating when he'd said he was tired. He'd left London at six o'clock that morning, stopped off at Stratford, and then come on up here. It had been a full-on day, especially the last few hours. That inviting bed sure was calling to him.

But first: Kate. He took out his phone and stared at it for a few moments. What to do? This business with Mrs Biscuit didn't sound good at all. He hoped the poor woman was going to manage to get a decent night's sleep. And the fact that Beth had asked him to stay had surprised and touched him. It was a measure of how badly she'd been shaken by the whole thing. She obviously trusted him, which could only be a good thing. Better that than scurrying away from him like a frightened rabbit, as she had earlier that afternoon in the churchyard. It might mean she'd sit and listen to what he had to say.

But that was for tomorrow's to-do list. At the top for today was Kate. He took a deep breath and called her number. She answered after two short rings.

'Hi, Joe. How's the trip going?' she said brightly.

'Fine. Stratford was great, but I'm up in the Lakes now, and things here are a bit more complicated than I expected. There's every chance I'm going to have to stay on another night.'

He heard her sharp intake of breath. 'You're not coming back tomorrow?'

'Maybe not. I thought I'd give you fair warning, just in case. It could be — '

'But you know how important this dinner is to me, Joe.' Her voice was ominously quiet.

'I know. And I'm sorry. If I can get things wrapped up here earlier, then I'll be there. I promise.'

'You promise? Now where have I heard that before?'

He swore silently to himself. He hated being on the defensive like this, but Kate was entitled to be annoyed. Which she obviously was. 'As I've already said, I'm really sorry. I'll do everything I can to wrap things up here as quickly as I can. And if I can get back in time, I will.'

'Big of you,' she said crisply.

'I've said I'm sorry. Something's happened, and — '

'This isn't working, Joe, is it?' she cut in again. 'You stood me up last week — '

'A board meeting overran. Hardly my fault. I did explain.'

'Yes, you always come up with a good explanation. Look, let's just forget about it, shall we?'

Joe sighed. 'Kate, I know you're cross with me, and you have every right to be. But can we talk this over when I get back? Truth to tell, I've had a hell of a day. I'll call you tomorrow, OK? And I'll try, really try, to get back in time for the dinner.'

'Don't bother,' she said briskly. 'Tomorrow is far too important for me to spend any of it worrying about whether or not you're going to make it.

So let's just say you won't and leave it at that. Best for both of us, I think.'

'Then I'll see you when I get back?'

There was a long pause. He could almost hear her taking a deep breath. 'No, I don't think so, Joe,' she said quietly, and ended the call.

Where had that come from? Joe sat for a long time staring at the phone. Well, that was him told. She sounded pretty annoyed, which was unusual for her. She wasn't one of those women who stamped her foot and screamed. It was one of the things he liked about her.

He made a note to get his PA to send her some flowers tomorrow. And he'd take her out to her favourite French restaurant when he got back by way of an apology. At least it meant he could stay around tomorrow and see this thing with Mrs Biscuit through. And there was that small matter of talking to Beth. He'd think about that tomorrow.

But sleep didn't come as easily as he'd thought. Just as he was drifting off, his treacherous mind took him back to the moment when Beth had stumbled and he'd held her in his arms. He remembered how soft her hair had felt against his chest; how well her head fitted into his shoulder.

Damn it. Damn it to hell. He sat bolt upright in bed, all chance of sleep blown out of the water. He knew he shouldn't have come back here. Stupid. Stupid, Stupid.

18

I didn't mean to oversleep. But the sleeplessness of the previous night, when I'd stayed up working on my profit forecast, must have caught up with me. I looked at the bedside clock in horror. How could I not have heard the alarm? Last night I'd told Mrs Biscuit that I'd do breakfast. And now everything was going to be late, and it was all my fault. I grabbed a pair of jeans and a sweatshirt, then rushed down to the kitchen, trying to ram my Brillo-Pad hair into a scrunchie as I did so. To my relief, Mrs Biscuit was already by the cooker.

'Mrs Biscuit, I'm so sorry. I must've slept through the alarm.'

'It's all right, pet,' she said in her usual calm voice, although the rings under her eyes told me she hadn't slept nearly as well as I had. 'Everything's under control here. Would you like some breakfast? Joe and Luke have already eaten and they've popped outside for a bit. Luke was keen to show off his skateboard.'

'There'll be more falling off than showing off, I imagine,' I said.

She gave a small smile, which was a start. 'Probably. Do you want breakfast? I can soon do you some.'

'It's OK, I'll grab some toast. I haven't got time for much else. But what are you doing here? I said I'd do breakfasts this morning. But what a good job you were, as it turns out.'

She reached into the bread bin, took out one of her lovely homemade loaves, and cut off a couple of slices. 'I'd rather keep busy,' she said as she dropped the slices into the toaster.

I could understand that. 'Have you heard how Mr Lawrence is this morning?'

'I phoned the hospital earlier.' She handed me the toast and a steaming mug of coffee. 'They said he'd had a comfortable night and had actually eaten something this morning. So that's good news, isn't it?'

'The best.' I felt a surge of relief as I spooned marmalade on the toast, suddenly ravenously hungry. 'Did they say if he's up to visitors?'

'I didn't ask. I just thought I'd turn up. Beth, about last night . . . ' Her fingers fretted away at the corner of her crisp white apron as her sweet round face puckered with anxiety. 'I feel dreadful about the way I snapped at you when you were only trying to be kind. I'll understand if you want me to leave — '

'Leave?' I nearly choked on my toast at the thought of it. 'Dear heaven, please, no.' I couldn't imagine Brackwith without her, and stretched out my hand to cover hers, which were cold in spite of the warmth of the kitchen. 'Honestly, you must believe me,' I said, desperate to reassure her. 'You've nothing to apologise for, I promise. You were shocked and upset. We all were.'

'And there's something I must tell you. It's about my last job and why I left.' She stopped as the phone rang. 'Shall I take that?'

'Please,' I mumbled through a mouthful of toast.

'Brackwith Guest House,' she said; then her face grew sombre as she listened. 'Oh, I see.' Her voice was quiet, guarded, a shade too polite, and it gave me a very bad feeling in the pit of my stomach. 'Yes, yes. We quite understand,' she went on. 'Well, thank you for letting us know.'

'What's wrong?' I asked as she stood staring at the phone as if it had just bitten her. 'Who was it?'

'It was Mrs Turner. You know, the party of ten booked in for next week?'

'The one we're doing the special dinner party for? Of course. I thought this afternoon we could make a start — '

'There's nothing to make a start on,' she said flatly. 'They've just cancelled. She said she'd heard we'd had an outbreak of food poisoning in the house, and as one of their party's been quite poorly recently, she didn't think it wise to take the risk.'

'You're kidding.' It was half-term next week and I'd turned away several people to accommodate the Turners, who'd taken over all our letting bedrooms for a special family get-together. I'd been hoping that the money we got from that booking would go some way to getting the builders to make some sort of start on the roof. 'But who said anything about food poisoning? Did Mrs Turner say how she knew?'

Mrs Biscuit shook her head. 'I didn't think to ask. I'm sorry. I should have done, shouldn't I?'

Yes, you damn well should have done, I wanted to shout. But one look at her stricken face and I was glad I'd bitten the words back. 'It's OK,' I said. 'But I'll just call her back.'

The booking form with her contact details was still on the dresser where I'd left it when it arrived in the post a couple of days ago. Filing is not one of my strong points, although it's a pretty safe bet that the sainted Miss Doble probably had a PhD in it.

'Mrs Turner? It's Beth here from Brackwith Guest House. You called earlier to cancel your booking.'

'Oh yes.' The woman's voice was wary, defensive. 'If there's a cancellation fee, I'll happily pay it. I'm sorry to let you down, but I can't take chances with my father-in-law's health. I'm sure you understand.'

'No, of course you can't. I understand completely. But that's not why I phoned. And please don't worry, there will be no cancellation fee.' Mr Horseface would probably call it poor business practice, but I was beyond caring.

'That's very kind of you,' she said, obviously still feeling awkward.

'Just one thing, though. You said you'd been told there was a case of food poisoning in the house?'

'Yes. Are you saying there isn't?

Because if so — '

'We don't know yet. It's true that one of our guests was taken ill last night, but we don't know the cause of that illness yet. Would you mind telling me who told you it was food poisoning?'

'The Environmental Health Department,' she said. 'Is there some mistake?'

'No,' I whispered as despair washed over me. 'No, Mrs Turner. There's no mistake.'

As I ended the call, Mrs Biscuit turned to me, her eyes glittering with tears. 'Oh lovey, this is all my fault. I'll be moving on as soon as I know Mr Lawrence is going to be OK.'

'But you can't leave.' I felt close to tears myself. 'I might as well sell the place now if you go.'

For the first time, I thought seriously about Simon's offer. It was, as he'd said yesterday, a generous one.

'I'll go and get Luke ready for school,' I said, and went outside to where he was showing off his skateboarding skills (or, rather, lack of them) to Joe. I looked out at the view of the valley that I'd known and loved for so long. I'd worked so hard to keep the dream alive. If Environmental Health closed us down, then it would all be for nothing. The end of my dream.

Joe came across to me, smiling. 'He's a great kid. A credit to you.'

'Thanks.' I forced some normality into my voice. 'He has his moments.'

'Thanks, too, for sending me the pictures of him. I really appreciate it.'

'You're Luke's only relative, you know,' I said, fighting hard against the urge to call out to Luke to be careful as he wobbled his way across the sloping yard. 'Apart from my mother — and — and yours, of course.'

'Wherever she may be.' He shrugged, then went back to watching Luke. 'He's just like Andrew was at that age. Did you know he's been on at me to take him climbing?'

My stomach coiled into a tight intricate knot. 'He's never said anything to me.'

'He said you'd say no.'

'He's not wrong there,' I said.

'He'd be a natural, you can tell that. His sense of balance is brilliant.'

'He's not going to be a climber,' I snapped.

'How are you going to stop him with all this on your doorstep?' Joe waved his arm. 'You've got one of the best beginners' scrambles in the Lake District right in your own backyard. I'm amazed he hasn't had a go already.'

The rocky outcrop at the back of the house was one of the reasons Andrew had been so keen to buy Brackwith, with the idea of setting up a climbing school. He'd once tried to teach me the basics, but nothing he taught me could change my conviction that the best way up a mountain was in a cable car. Skinning knees, knuckles and any other sticky-outy bits on razor-sharp rock was definitely not my thing.

But Joe was telling me it was Luke's? 'He wouldn't dare.' As I spoke, I realised Joe had given me the best reason — indeed, the only valid reason — for turning my back on my dream and accepting Simon's client's offer. 'And don't you go putting ideas in his head. I've already lost one person I love to the mountains.'

And if you hadn't dragged Andrew off climbing that day, he'd still be alive. The thought flashed through my head, but I pushed it back. If Joe and I were going to get into the blame game about Andrew's death, there was no way I was going to come out of it unscathed.

'Beth.' Joe put his hand on my arm, and there was an edge of something in his voice I'd never heard before. 'About Andrew's accident. I need to . . . well, the thing is, I've got to — '

'Please, Joe, it was all a long time ago now,' I said quickly, stepping away from him and calling for Luke to come on in.

I knew it had been a mistake for Joe to come, raking up things that were better left alone. I'd got it all sorted in my mind until he came along and unsorted them all, reminding me of all the things

I should have said seven years ago. I'd bottled out then — and I was bottling out now.

Everything whirled around my head like socks in a tumble drier. Joe, Andrew, Mr Lawrence, the Environmental Health. The Turners cancelling, not to mention the worry about how I was going to pay next month's mortgage with no money coming in. See what happens when you take your head out of the sand? Complete chaos. All I wanted to do at that moment was get my head out of that tumble drier and back into the nearest sand dune.

'I'm sorry, Joe; I'm really busy at the moment.' I turned to go back indoors. Not a sand dune, but better than nothing. 'I've got to get Luke to school.'

'Then at least let me help you.'

'Help me?' I paused, my hand on the doorknob, and made a feeble attempt to lighten the moment. 'In what way? Are you offering to cook if Mrs Biscuit up and leaves? Which she's threatening to do, by the way, on top of everything else. Like I don't have enough to worry about.'

'Oh, I don't think she will,' he said with a certainty that I wished I shared. 'Look, Beth, I know you're having problems. The water marks on the ceiling are a bit of a giveaway. That and the sagging roof line. You know, Andrew wouldn't have wanted you to work yourself to death the way you do.'

'How would you know?' I asked sharply.

'Because I knew Andrew. If things got tricky, he had this habit of shrugging his shoulders and walking away.'

Tricky? Things between me and Andrew had got as tricky as they could get. Andrew didn't walk away from me; he ran — as far and as fast as he could. And if I hadn't pushed him, hadn't screamed back at him and said all those awful things, he wouldn't have gone storming off like that.

'Beth? Did you hear me?' Joe asked. 'I said I could advance you as much money as you need to maintain Brackwith. And before you go all proud and starchy on me, it can be a straightforward loan, or I'll take a stake in the business, whichever you prefer. Call it an investment in Luke's future if you like. This place has terrific potential, and I know you and Andrew had some great plans for the outbuildings.'

'I don't need your money,' I said quickly. 'It's very kind of you, but I've decided to sell Brackwith. You're right, Andrew wouldn't have wanted me to work myself to death trying to keep it together. It's time I moved on with my life. Now, excuse me; Miss Doble will put me in the naughty corner if I'm late again. Luke, will you come in at once!' I yelled as I scurried into the house.

Luke and Joe came in a few minutes later. 'Mummy, make Joe stay,' Luke pleaded. 'He was going to take me climbing tomorrow. Now he says he's got to go. Tell him he mustn't.'

'I can't do that,' I said, avoiding Joe's eye. 'He's a busy man.'

I didn't wait to hear what Joe's answer was, but bustled around getting Luke ready for school, only half-listening as he reminded me that today was Friday and that school finished at lunchtimes on a Friday.

'I know,' I said when he'd reminded me for the fifth time.

'But sometimes you forget.'

'Not today,' I said with my fingers firmly crossed. It was only a very tiny white lie, and I would have remembered the minute I got to school.

'And I'm always the last in the playground. Miss Doble says — '

'Just get in the car, Luke, otherwise you'll be late for school. And *then* what will Miss Doble say?'

19

I dropped Luke off and grovelled to Miss Doble as I handed in the missing note for the school trip which had somehow (I avoided Luke's eyes as I said this) slipped down the back of the dresser. Normally this would have made me feel the worst of all Bad Mothers, but that morning my mind was too full of the conversation with Joe.

I pulled up sharply when I heard someone call my name, then cursed myself for stopping. My heart sank at the sight of Fiona Farrington-Smythe advancing towards me across the playground like a galleon in full sail.

'Beth, I'm so glad I caught you,' she said. 'You're terribly hard to pin down, you know.'

'Pin down,' two of her acolytes echoed in perfect harmony, like they were auditioning to be her backing group.

'I'm sorry, but I'm in a bit of a rush now, to be honest,' I said. 'And my car's on double yellows — '

'This won't take long. I was just wondering if we could bank on that little lady who does your catering for you to bake us a cake or two for the school fayre next weekend?'

I wasn't sure Mrs Biscuit would approve of being described as a 'little lady who caters' for me. Nor, I thought, would she be in the mood for baking. At least, not until the news about Mr Lawrence was better. Not to mention the inevitable visit from Environmental Health.

'Well, she's pretty busy at the moment,' I said, and blanched as Queen Fiona turned the full force of her eyes on me so that I knew what a mouse felt like when cornered by a hungry cat. 'I — I'll ask her,' I added, cursing myself for being such a coward as I almost ran out of the playground.

But it was obviously my day for being waylaid, because as I reached my car a man stepped out of the shadows and came towards me.

'Simon, what are you doing here?' I was completely thrown by the sight of him. Even though I'd sort of decided to accept his client's offer, I wasn't quite ready to tell him that. So before he had chance to refer to it, I clicked open my car door. 'Look, I'm sorry, but I really am in a terrible rush.'

'It's all right; I won't keep you long. But this is urgent.'

'So urgent you couldn't phone?'

'Too important to say over the phone,' he said. 'And I knew I'd find you here at this time of the morning. Firstly, I've come to apologise for upsetting you yesterday.'

'Oh no, really.' I got into the driver's seat and put the key in the ignition. 'There was nothing — '

'And secondly,' he cut across, his voice smooth as a snake, 'I've found out a couple of things you ought to know. I hear Joe Tennant is staying with you. Did you know he's up here on a buying trip?'

Miss Doble would, I know, have said something haughty and dignified about not listening to gossip. But she was made of sterner stuff than me. In spite of myself, I was intrigued. 'Buying what?' I couldn't help asking.

'You know he owns a chain of small upmarket country hotels?'

'Yes, of course I do.'

'Well, I've heard he's actively seeking to expand.' Simon eyes gleamed, knowing full well he'd reeled me in like a curious catfish. 'And Brackwith is exactly the type of property he's looking for, according to my people. Reasonably sized house in need of modernisation, loads of outbuildings, superb location. The place ticks all his boxes and then some.'

'You're not saying he's your mystery buyer?' I felt a chill of horror at the thought of it.

Simon shook his head. 'Hardly. Well, come on — I can see it in your face that

I'm bang on target. He's made you an offer, hasn't he? It explains what he's doing up here after all this time. Why he's suddenly developed an interest in his nephew after how many years? And, like I said, Brackwith is exactly his sort of property. Check out his company's website if you don't believe me.'

I drew in a sharp breath as I recalled Joe's offer to 'take a stake in the business' and felt anger begin to churn my insides. How dare he act like he was doing me this stonking great favour, when all the time he was merely seeking to expand his property portfolio. Andrew always said Joe could be ruthless, but until that moment I'd not realised quite how ruthless. And to use Luke and that train set as a cover story . . . Unbelievable. And last night I'd started thinking that maybe he wasn't so bad after all. I'd actually felt safe and protected when he'd put his arms around me. I'd felt . . . What a fool I'd almost made of myself. Along with the anger, I could feel my face burn.

If I had to sell Brackwith, Joe Tennant would be the last person on earth I'd sell to. Suddenly, Simon's client and his breathtaking offer sounded a lot less offensive.

'Ah yes. I see he has,' Simon said with a shake of his head. 'Well, whatever it was, I'm sure my client would more than match it. Like I said, he's very keen.'

'I — I can't . . . ' My knuckles had gone white where I was gripping the steering wheel so tightly. I still couldn't quite bring myself to say that I'd accept his client's offer. And yet . . . and yet . . .

'And there's something else you should know,' Simon pressed on, knowing he had my full attention. 'About the woman you call Mrs Biscuit.'

I started the car. Just when I was beginning to think he wasn't so bad after all, he had to start having a go at Mrs Biscuit again. What was it with him?

'If you mean that's not her real

name,' I said icily, 'I know. It's Ivy Biston. She made no secret of it. It was Luke's idea to call her Mrs Biscuit.'

'Then did you also know that this same Ivy Biston used to work as a cook at a well-known private school? That she was sacked, and the only reason the police weren't involved was because the school didn't want word to get out?'

'I told you, I'm not interested in what she may or may not have done.' I'd had enough of Simon's malicious gossip, and it served me right for encouraging him. Besides, I wanted to get away before the anger I felt towards Joe spilled over and I'd end up saying or doing something I'd regret. 'I trust her implicitly.'

'Even with your son's life?' Until that moment, I hadn't realised how much his thin, pale face resembled a weasel's. 'She was accused of poisoning a thirteen-year-old girl, did you know that? Thankfully the child recovered, otherwise the school would have had no choice but to involve the police.'

'It sounds like some horrible kind of accident.'

'An accident?' His thin, sandy eyebrows lifted. 'Well, 'accidents' seem to have a habit of following that woman around, don't they? I hear one of your guests is in hospital with suspected poisoning. I'm right, aren't I?'

'Well, it — it's true Mr Lawrence collapsed last night and was taken into hospital. Yes,' I floundered. 'But they haven't completed all the tests — '

'As for that 'accident' in the school,' he went on, 'there's no point asking her about it. It appears your Ivy Biston can't remember a thing.'

I shook my head. 'She wouldn't — '

Once again, he cut across me. He leaned into the car, his face inches away from my own. 'Your precious Mrs Biscuit has, it turns out, a bit of an alcohol problem.'

'Now you're being totally ridiculous, Simon.' My patience snapped. 'Step away from the car, please.'

'I'm only telling you for your own

good,' he said, then jumped away quickly as I slammed the car in gear and roared up the road.

20

Joe watched Beth's car until it disappeared down the bumpy track and out of sight. Then he turned and went back into the kitchen, where Mrs Biscuit was clearing up the remains of breakfast.

'I've got to tell her, Joe,' she said abruptly, shutting the door of the dishwasher with a thump. 'I should have done so right from the beginning. I hate all this lying and secrecy.'

'I know you do, Ivy, and I'm sorry now that I asked you to keep it quiet.' He picked up the coffee pot and poured out two mugs, one of which he pushed across the table towards her, and gestured for her to sit down. 'I just thought it best for Beth and Luke to keep things simple at this stage. You know how prickly she can be.'

Ivy Biston sighed. 'Tell me about it.' She sat down at the table opposite him and picked up the mug. 'Thanks. I'm ready for this.'

'Me too,' he said with a grimace, his head still reeling from the encounter with Beth. 'So she's been prickly with you as well?'

She nodded. 'I offered her some financial help a while back, when this trouble with the roof first started. She nearly bit my head off — in an icily polite way, if you know what I mean.'

Joe didn't exactly. There had been precious little politeness, icy or otherwise, in the way she'd responded to his offer. 'Then the sooner I can persuade her to sell up this money pit, the better. Then she can get on with her life.'

'I don't think it's your place to do that,' Mrs Biscuit said firmly. 'It's got to be her decision.'

'Except she's not thinking straight at the moment, Ivy. This thing with Mr Lawrence has really shaken her.' His heart went out to the troubled woman sitting opposite him. Her face paled, making the dark circles under her eyes even more pronounced. She appeared to have aged ten years in the last twenty-four hours.

'It's shaken me, too, I don't mind telling you,' she said, putting her coffee down untasted. 'Then when I heard the Environmental Health Department have got involved already, before they've even found out for sure what's wrong with him . . . It's terrible. You'd think they'd have been in touch with us here before they started contacting our customers, wouldn't you?'

'They did?' Joe stared at her. 'Are you sure?'

'It's hardly the sort of thing I'd make up now, is it?' she snapped, then sighed. 'I'm sorry, I didn't mean to bark at you like that. It was a party of ten that cancelled. They were going to take over the entire house for a whole week, which would've relieved the pressure on the financial side of things. Beth can hardly afford to lose that big a booking on top of everything else.'

Joe glanced at his watch. 'Look, I'm

going to head off. I've got things to do this morning, and I don't think Beth is that keen on me being here when she gets back.'

'But I thought you two were getting on better? You seemed more at ease with each other last night.'

Joe thought back to the moment when Beth had, just for a second, allowed herself to relax into his arms. 'We were,' he said, 'until I messed up. Look, I've got to go. I'll be in touch.'

'So I'm going to tell her, OK?' Ivy looked determined.

Joe sighed. It was all going to come crashing down around his ears now. Well, so be it. He'd handle it.

'Yes, you'd better tell her. And you can tell her too that it was all my idea, and that I thought I was acting in her best interests.'

'Why don't you tell her that yourself?' Ivy asked.

'Because she wouldn't believe me.'

'True. But then, once I tell her the truth, she isn't going to believe it coming from me either, is she?'

Joe shook his head. 'Probably not.'

'Just promise me one thing, Joe, because of course I won't be staying after this. I've grown very fond of Beth and would hate to see her hurt, and I'm still worried about that Simon sniffing around. I wouldn't trust him further than I could throw him. So you will keep an eye on her, won't you — from a distance this time, eh?'

Joe shrugged on his coat and felt in his pocket for his car keys. He looked around the warm, cosy kitchen with genuine regret at the realisation that he was probably seeing it for the last time. 'Yeah,' he said with a sigh. 'From a distance might be best. For all of us.'

Then he went out, remembering as he did so to give the sticking front door a kick in the right place.

21

During the journey back to Brackwith, I focused on my driving and tried to push the thought of what I'd like to do and say to Joe Tennant if he was still there to the back of my mind. But it wouldn't stay there, and when I turned the car in through the gates of the house, I was in some perverse way disappointed to find that his car was no longer parked in the collecting yard. I was just in the mood to give him a well-deserved piece of my mind.

As for Mrs Biscuit, I'd already decided I wasn't even going to mention Simon's ridiculous allegations to her. She had enough to deal with at the moment. This kind, funny lady who'd brought order to my chaotic kitchen, kept my business going when it was on its knees, and even managed to persuade Luke to eat broccoli, was the best friend I'd ever had. The idea she could have harmed anyone, least of all a child, was ludicrous. And I never believed it for one single second. Simon had never liked her and he was simply being malicious.

She was in the kitchen when I got back, not busy cooking for once but sitting at the table, her usually busy hands clasped in her lap, her face sombre. 'I'm off to the hospital in a minute,' she said without looking up. 'But first I've got something to tell you. I tried to earlier, but then Mrs Turner rang to cancel and the moment passed. It's about why I left my last job.'

My heart gave an uncomfortable lurch as I sat opposite her. Just one look at her face told me this was something deadly serious. Surely there wasn't some truth in Simon's nonsense? 'Before you say any more,' I said quickly, anxious to reassure her, 'I want you to know that you don't have to go to the hospital on your own. I'm coming with you. Just give me five minutes to collect some things. As for why you left your last job, you don't have to — '

'Yes, Beth. Yes I do. Just hear me out.' Her eyes glinted with determination and I could see her take a deep breath before speaking. 'I — I left because one of the pupils became ill after eating a slice of my cake, which was found to contain laburnum seeds.'

'But you didn't put them there, surely?'

'Of course I didn't. One of the other children did. She thought it would just give the girl a tummy ache and had no idea how dangerous the seeds could be to an asthma sufferer, as her unfortunate victim was.'

'That sounds like a childish prank that went horribly wrong,' I said, hugely relieved that my first reaction had been the right one. Simon had, indeed, got it wrong. 'It wasn't your fault.'

'But it was.' She clasped and unclasped her hands. 'You see, I'd had a couple of sherries with my lunch, a foolish habit I'd slipped into since my Norman died. To be honest, it was rather more than a couple, and I nodded off. I have vague memories of the girl coming into the kitchen, but nothing more.'

'Was the girl found out?'

Mrs Biscuit shook her head.

I looked at her closely. 'You didn't tell anyone, did you? Why? Why take the blame when it cost you your job?'

'She wasn't a bad girl, just a silly one who'd been teased by the other girl beyond endurance. She was desperately upset and frightened and will never do anything so foolish again, of that I am absolutely certain. As for it costing me my job, I was going to leave anyway. And it was my fault, you know. If I'd been fully awake that afternoon when she came into the kitchen, it would never have happened. I haven't had a drop of alcohol from that day. Nor ever will.'

So that explained why she'd refused the glass of sherry so vehemently the night before. It also explained some-thing else. 'And so that's how you knew Mr Lawrence had been poisoned.'

She nodded. 'I'm no doctor, but it occurred to me that the symptoms were identical. At the hospital last night I insisted they test for laburnum poison-ing, so he got the correct treatment quickly, thank goodness. Only now I've got this horrible feeling they suspect me, which is why I want to take the pies in for analysis. I'd hardly do that if I was a poisoner, would I?'

'Of course you wouldn't,' I said. 'But I don't get it. How could laburnum, or any other poison, have got in the pie? Surely it's more likely he picked up some seeds while he was out and about and ate them without realising what they were.'

She frowned. 'I've been wondering that. It doesn't seem very likely though, does it? He spends most of his time up on the fells bird-watching. And you don't get too many laburnum tree up here, do you?'

Gardening wasn't my strong point. 'I have no idea. What do they look like?'

'They're sometimes called 'golden chain' because they have long strings of bright yellow flowers in the spring. There's a row of them in that park in town where Luke sometimes goes skateboarding. Do you know where I mean?'

I shook my head. 'No, sorry. But then I can't think straight at the moment. You found the pies, I take it? Luckily Joe stopped me throwing them away.'

'I did. And I've taken the remains of Mr Lawrence's pie out of the bin. I'll take them all.'

'Right then.' I went towards the door. 'I'll just go and get ready. Shan't be a moment.'

'Beth?' she called. 'You do know he's gone, do you?'

'Who?'

'Joe, of course. He's gone.'

My face hardened. 'Good. I've got enough problems without him adding to them.'

'He's one of the good guys,' she said. 'Whatever it is you think he's done, he's always had your best interests at heart.'

'You reckon?' I snorted.

'I know,' she said firmly.

'I've just found out why he's here.' My voice shook as the anger, never far from the surface, bubbled up. 'He wants to buy Brackwith and turn it into one of his fancy bloody hotels, filled with Hooray Henrys in Mulberry jackets racketing around in their four-wheel drives. They'll probably insist on a cable car up to the tarn.'

'Don't be ridiculous.' Mrs Biscuit pushed her chair back and stood up to face me. Her cheeks were as flushed as mine as we faced each other like two pumped-up boxers waiting for the bell. 'I've known Joe for years. He's a good, kind man and would never — '

'You've what?'

The ticking of the clock on the dresser was the only sound that broke the tense silence that had suddenly fallen.

'I've known him for years,' she said eventually. 'I used to work for him.'

I couldn't believe it. 'But when he came here yesterday, you acted like you didn't know each other. Now you're saying you've known him for years?' Then I remembered the easy way she'd called him 'Joe'. It had seemed out of character at the time, but it made perfect sense now. 'And are you still working for him?'

I thought she'd deny it; say I was being ridiculous again. But she didn't. Instead, she broke eye contact and looked down at the table. She put a hand out and scratched at a tiny spot there.

22

'In a manner of speaking, yes.' Her voice was so quiet I had to strain to hear.

'Would you care to explain?' I was hurt; angry. I'd trusted her; defended her against Simon's allegations, when all the time . . .

'Norman — that's my late husband — and I used to own a pub over towards Keswick,' she said in such a low voice I had to strain to hear. 'We — we'd known Joe and Andrew for years, since they were scarcely more than boys. They'd come into the pub whenever they were climbing in the area. Well, to cut a long story short, a few years ago Norman and I ran into financial difficulties. We'd had some work done on the pub which, to be honest, we simply couldn't afford, and the bank called in the overdraft. We were pretty down about it one day and told Joe, who offered to buy us out.'

'That seems to be a favourite ploy of his,' I muttered, but she ignored me.

'He was so good to us,' she went on, still scratching away at that same spot on the table. 'He let us stay on and run the place, which we did, until Norman's heart attack. And when Norman died, I didn't want to stay there on my own. Joe wanted to find me somewhere else in one of his other places, but this job at the school came up. Then when the trouble came, the school wanted me to leave quietly. But it got into the papers anyway, as the parents of the girl who was poisoned went to the press. Not that I blame them, of course. Joe read about it and came to see me.'

'And offered you a job?' I had a bad feeling I knew what her answer was going to be. 'It was to do with me, wasn't it?'

'I'm sorry.' Her voice shook. 'He said you'd be annoyed if you found out.'

'Annoyed? That's one word for it.' In

fact I didn't have words to describe how I felt, although if I had, then cheated and betrayed would have been pretty near the top of the list. I'd trusted her and thought her my friend.

'What was your brief?' My voice was edged with bitterness. 'To report back to him when the state of my finances reached a level where he could come in with an offer I couldn't refuse?'

'Right. That's it.' She heaved herself up, more angry than I'd ever seen her, her face scarlet, her eyes fierce. 'Time for a few homes truths, young lady. Joe was looking out for you, just as he always looked out for Andrew — something he's been doing since their mother skipped off to Spain with her fancy man, and their fool of a father dealt with it by drinking himself to death. Did you know Joe stayed home to run the family hotel so Andrew could go to university, so that he could have all the chances Joe never had? Chances which, needless to say, being Andrew, he squandered.'

I caught my breath. Andrew had always moaned that their father had left the hotel to Joe because he was 'the favoured one'. He'd also boasted that uni had been one long party and that he'd scraped through on the minimum of work.

'I was always telling Joe he did too much,' she went on, as if now she'd started she was unable to stop. 'That he should let Andrew sort out his own messes. But he wouldn't — '

'Is that how he sees me and Luke?' I cut in. 'Another of Andrew's messes?'

She shook her head. 'You don't get it, do you? He's eaten up with guilt about the accident. He blames himself for Andrew's death.'

'Blames himself? You reckon?' I gave a bitter laugh. 'You've got that all wrong. He blames me, more like. You should see the way he looks at me sometimes. I saw him by Andrew's grave after the funeral, you know. He looked up and saw me. He was so angry, like he hated the sight of me.

Then there was that song. He did it just to wind me up.'

Once again my head filled with the sound of Queen belting out 'Don't Stop Me Now', as it had the day of the funeral — and still, even after all these years, it felt like someone had slammed their fist into my stomach.

'Do you mean 'Don't Stop Me Now'? That wasn't down to Joe. In fact it was a couple of his climbing mates who'd suggested it to the vicar. They were talking about it at the wake. Didn't you hear them?'

'I — I wasn't there,' I said, feeling more than a little guilty. Not to mention foolish.

'And there's one more thing you got wrong about that day, Beth,' she said. 'Joe was angry, all right. Still is, poor chap. But not with you.'

'Then who?'

'Himself. Who do you think? He won't talk about it, but one of the rescuers said he'd told them he and Andrew had this big row up on Crinkle

Crag. And — well, you know the rest.'

Andrew and Joe had a row? The mood Andrew was in when he left, it wouldn't surprise me. And that, too, was my fault. I had a sudden sick feeling in my stomach. 'What did they row about?' I asked.

Mrs Biscuit shrugged. 'How would I know? I was hardly going to ask him, was I, now?'

'But Andrew's accident was my fault, not Joe's. That's why I thought Joe was angry with me,' I whispered. 'I thought Andrew had told him . . . ' I stopped. I owed it to Joe for him to be the first to hear about that last, terrible row Andrew and I had had that day. How he'd screamed that Joe had been right about me all along, that I was a spoilt brat who schemed and manipulated to get what I wanted. That I'd got pregnant deliberately (not true) and refused to have an abortion (true) so that I could trap him even further (so, so not true). How I'd turned my face away from his last kiss.

If I'd known, that day at the graveside, that Joe blamed himself for the accident, I'd have summoned up the courage to have told him, even though I'd always been a little afraid of him. I had always been aware that he disapproved of me; thought me shallow and selfish and not a suitable wife for his brother. He'd never been at any great pains to hide it.

'And while we're into home truths,' Mrs Biscuit went on, 'where do you think the money came from that was paid into your account yesterday?'

'You? Oh no, you shouldn't have —'

'Not me. But I told Joe you were having problems with the bank. He's been keeping his eye on you all these years, you know; checking with that woman who worked here before me.'

'Sally?' I stared at her in astonishment. Mrs Biscuit, and before her, Sally, both checking up on me? Both reporting back to Joe? 'But she never said —'

'Then, when she left, that's when he

sent me here. His way of making amends, as he saw it; that's what I reckoned. Anyway, it was Joe who paid the money into your account this week.'

'But why didn't he tell me?'

'You'll have to ask him that.' She looked at her watch. 'I've got to get to the hospital. But there's one last thing you need to know. Joe isn't up here to buy your house. He came because I asked him to. Because I was worried about you.'

I didn't answer. Just sat there, staring at the same spot on the table that she had done. Mrs Biscuit, the woman I'd trusted, had let into my home, my family. I had allowed myself and Luke to get fond of her, when all the time she was working for Joe. Reporting to him on the state of my finances. Summoning him when she thought I was in so deep there was no way back. My head was reeling.

'I'll clear out my things when I get back,' she said quietly. 'I think it's for the best all round, don't you?'

I nodded and didn't even look up as she put the pies in her basket and went out, the front door screeching in protest as she kicked it shut behind her.

23

Ivy was still shaking when she reached the hospital, which made reversing the car into a tight spot in the busy car park even more of a trial than usual. She must have driven here on autopilot while she agonised over the conversation with Beth. If only she'd told her right from the start about the poisoning at the school and her part in it, she wouldn't have given her the job, and poor Mr Lawrence wouldn't be here in the hospital. Everything, but everything, was her fault.

As for telling Beth about her connection with Joe, she should at the very least have come clean about that after she'd asked Joe to come up here. She shouldn't have kept putting it off, waiting for the 'right moment'. She'd intended to confide in Mr Lawrence and ask his advice on what she should do. It was one of the reasons she'd agreed to go to the concert with him. That, and to get away from the difficulty of pretending not to know Joe, of course.

But then Mr Lawrence had been taken ill — was that only last night? It seemed months ago now. The memory of the way he'd groaned and doubled over would haunt her forever.

Thank goodness Joe had been there. Who knew how she and Beth would have coped if Joe hadn't taken control of the situation. He really was one of the best, was Joe, which was why she'd got so mad just now when she heard Beth run him down like that. The girl had a blind spot about him and that was a fact.

She picked up her basket, locked the car and, on legs that felt as if they'd turned to jelly, walked into the hospital. At first she had problems finding anyone who knew what she was talking about. What had she expected — a reception committee waiting to whisk her pies off to the laboratory and her to the nearest police cell? But eventually a harassed-looking receptionist made some phone calls, then took the pies away, leaving Ivy with a bizarre sense of anticlimax. What would happen now? There was no one around to ask.

Her shoes squeaked on the polished floors as she made her way along the endless corridors to the ward where Mr Lawrence had been taken last night, hoping he'd still be in the same place. She needed to see him, to reassure herself that he really was going to be all right before she left the area for good. He was in a room with three other beds and, if her memory served her right, his was just inside the door.

To her relief, he was indeed still there. And, better than that, he was sitting up, doing the *Telegraph* crossword. He was still wearing the hospital gown from the night before, and although he looked very pale, he no longer had an oxygen mask on. His face lit up as he saw her.

'Mrs Biscuit! Ivy.' He put the paper down and beamed at her. 'How lovely to see you. So kind of you to come in.'

'Not so kind, Mr Lawrence — '

'It's John, please,' he said with that sweet, gentle smile of his. 'How many times do I have to ask you that?'

'Very well . . . John.' She gave him a wobbly smile in return. 'I've — I've just come to apologise, and then I'll be on my way.'

He looked puzzled. 'Dear lady, you have nothing to apologise for.'

'Well, I should have brought you in a pair of pyjamas for a start,' she said, ever the practical one. 'I'm afraid I wasn't thinking too straight this morning.'

That had to be the understatement of the year, she thought ruefully, as the upsetting scene in Beth's kitchen flashed through her mind once again.

'Please don't worry about it,' he said. 'Though if you could do so the next time you come in, that would be wonderful. Assuming there is a next time, of course. There, now — apology accepted.'

'Oh no, that wasn't it,' she said hastily. 'I'm apologising for the pie. For poisoning you. At least, that seems to be what they think happened.'

He shook his head. 'But you didn't poison me. Whatever happened, it was an accident.'

'Haven't the police been to see you yet?' Ivy asked. 'Or the Environmental Health people? They've already been in contact with one of Beth's customers.'

'I haven't had any visitors at all. But then, the sister in charge of the ward is a bit of a dragon by all accounts. I'm surprised you managed to slip past her.'

'Oh, I'm sorry.' She turned to look down the corridor towards the still-deserted nurses' station. 'There was no one around when I came in just now. I'd best go then. I didn't realise — '

'No, no, please don't,' he said. 'I really am feeling so much better now the medication's kicked in. In fact I'm rather hungry, and could do with some of your lovely home cooking.' He looked hopefully at her basket. 'I don't suppose you've brought anything, by any chance?'

Her eyes prickled with tears. 'I don't think I'll ever cook anything ever again and that's a fact. I've brought nothing but trouble on poor Beth and you. And . . . ' Suddenly the strain of the last day took its toll, and the tears which had refused to come last night in the privacy of her bedroom spilled over in this very public place and trickled, unchecked, down her face. She was aware of the man in the bed opposite looking at them with undisguised interest, but couldn't help herself.

'Oh my dear, please don't be upset.' John Lawrence looked as distressed as she felt. 'As for you bringing trouble, you couldn't be more wrong. Come and sit down, I beg you.'

He put his newspaper on the locker and motioned her towards the grey plastic chair by the side of his bed. She started to speak, but he held up his hand to stop her.

'No, listen to me, please. It's important. I've been going over and over this in my mind while I've been lying here, and if I don't say it now, I'll probably never find the courage again.' He took a deep breath and looked at her intently, his twinkly blue eyes unusually serious. 'And I apologise in advance if what I'm about to say embarrasses you. You see, when my wife passed away five years ago, I thought that nothing would ever make me happy again — apart from the bird-watching, maybe. But part of the attraction of even that, I now realise, was that it's such a solitary pastime.'

Ivy blinked away her tears, her heart thudding. Beth was always teasing her that Mr Lawrence — John — was sweet on her. Could it be that she was right? And if so, how did she feel about that? After her Norman, she'd thought she was past all that nonsense. But there was this strange fluttery feeling in her stomach that was probably due to the fact that she'd forgotten to have break-fast that morning. And yet . . . She held her breath and waited for him to carry on speaking.

'As for wanting to spend time with another person,' he went on, 'that was completely out of the question. Until, that is, I met you.'

She gulped, and the fluttering in her stomach became the dance of a thousand butterflies.

'I've shocked you, I can see that, and I apologise if I'm talking out of turn,' he went on when she didn't (although the truth was, she couldn't) answer. 'I've been wanting to speak out for some time now but kept putting it off. But being in this place has given me plenty of time to think about it. About seizing the day and all that.'

'Mr Lawrence — I mean, John . . . ' Ivy twisted her hands together, those butterflies now doing a conga not only in her stomach but in her chest and throat as well. 'I really don't know — '

'I shouldn't have said anything,' he said quickly. 'Please don't fret. I'm so sorry.'

'No, no,' she said, anxious to reassure him, 'it was just unexpected, that's all. I came here expecting to find that you blamed me for poisoning you, and — '

'As I've already said, I don't for a minute believe it was anything you did that caused my collapse,' he said. 'In fact, your wonderful cooking has given me my life back. Before I came up here, I'd completely lost all interest in eating, or anything. Ivy, my dear, you have brought nothing but joy into my life and that's the truth.'

Ivy flushed with pleasure. But her smile soon faded as the fear, never far from her mind, resurfaced. 'Oh John, you don't know the half of it. They've called in the Environmental Health officers, you know, who said the pie that you ate was poisoned. Beth's going to be shut down and it's all my fault.'

'How can it be your fault?' he asked. 'You didn't put poison in the pie, did you?'

'Of course I didn't.'

'Then how did the poison, if indeed that's what it was, get in the pie? Have you asked yourself that?'

Ivy stared at him. It hadn't even

occurred to her.

'Well, that's what the police should be focusing on, don't you think?' he said. 'Always assuming they need to be involved at all. What's much more likely is that I had a severe allergic reaction to something. As far as I'm aware, that's what they've been testing for. I'm asthmatic, you know, and I do get these odd reactions to things now and again.'

She clasped her hands together. 'An allergic reaction. That would be wonderful — ' she began, then checked herself. 'Oh no, I'm sorry. I didn't mean — '

'I know exactly what you meant.' He smiled.

'And you're right, of course,' she went on. 'It couldn't have been a deliberate poisoning, could it? Maybe there was something wrong with the meat? Yet the butcher I use is the best in the area. It's simply not possible.'

Nevertheless, she felt as if a huge weight had rolled off her shoulders. She knew she hadn't knowingly put anything untoward in the pie, and she was the only one who'd touched it. It must have been an allergic reaction, as he'd said.

'Thank you,' she said. 'I can't tell you what a relief that is. I thought . . . I really thought I'd poisoned you.'

'But why on earth would you think such a thing? I rather think you've been reading too many Agatha Christies, my dear.'

Ivy's smile faded. Should she tell him about the poisoning at the school? She'd put off telling Beth, and look where that had got her. 'There's something I should — ' she began when he spoke at the same time.

'I wonder if I can ask a huge favour — '

'Go on,' she said, grateful for a bit of time in which to choose her words more carefully.

'Very well. I was about to say they're talking of letting me go home, provided there's someone to look after me. Do you think . . . I mean, will Beth let me come back to Brackwith? Will you have a word with her? I assure you I do not need looking after. I'll be no trouble, I promise.'

'Of course I will. And I'm sure her answer will be yes, of course. But the thing is, I won't be — '

'What are you doing here?' a voice that could have been used to direct shipping in the Channel boomed out, making them both jump. 'Who are you?'

Ivy whirled round, and there was the ward sister, the size of her voice at complete variance to her small birdlike frame. She was a short wiry woman with a helmet of stiff greying hair and a clipboard clasped to her thin chest. Her mouth was set in a hard line, and she looked every inch the dragon of her reputation, reminding Ivy of a character from one of Luke's reading books. She half-expected to see fire coming out of her quivering nostrils.

'I'm — I'm sorry,' Ivy stammered. 'There was no one at the nurses' station when I arrived.'

'That's because it's not official visiting time,' the dragon snapped. 'Come back at two o'clock.'

'But I won't be here then. I have to go away. That's what I came here to tell Mr Lawrence.'

'Are you a relative?'

'No,' Ivy said while at the same time John Lawrence said, 'Yes. Yes she is.'

Ivy stood up to go. 'I'll be back later,' she said.

'Is that a promise?' John asked, his eyes never leaving her face.

She flushed. 'I — I promise I'll be back.'

'Remember you agreed to ask Beth? And you'll not leave the area? I need to know, Ivy,' he prompted when she didn't answer.

'I'll not leave without telling you, John,' she said softly, savouring the way his name felt on her tongue.

She touched his hand lightly, then left the ward, her heart singing. He was going to be all right. In fact, better than all right. The poisoning was just a figment of her fevered imagination. It was just an allergic reaction, that was all. And maybe, just maybe . . .

On lighter feet, she began the long walk down the featureless corridor that led towards the lifts, then stopped dead. Two uniformed policemen were coming towards her, their faces grim. She turned away and began to walk in the other direction, trying hard not to draw attention to herself by hurrying. But before she could take a few steps, she heard someone call her name.

'Mrs Biscuit? Ivy? Please wait.' It was Beth.

She turned around, and as she did so, saw the two policemen exchange glances. They came towards her.

'Are you Mrs Ivy Biston?' the taller of the two asked.

Ivy felt like a child who'd been given an ice cream, only to have it snatched away before she could take even one small bite. She had a very bad feeling she knew exactly what that grim-faced policeman was going to say next.

24

I sat at the kitchen table, sick and ashamed of myself, only half-aware of Mrs Biscuit leaving. Until, that is, I heard the screech of the front door as she kicked it shut. I called after her but I was too late; she'd already gone. Perhaps it wasn't such a bad thing, though. Best to talk to her later, by which time I'd be a bit better at being able to express myself and apologise properly.

But before that, I needed to speak to Joe. Urgently.

I began to dial his number, but cancelled the call as my nerve failed me. Besides, this wasn't something I could do over the phone. I'd have to go and see him. The trouble was, I had no idea where he'd gone. He could have left the area for all I knew. I gave myself a good talking-to, took a deep breath, and dialled his number again. All I had to do was say I needed to see him and arrange to meet him somewhere if he was still around. What was so hard about that?

But my carefully rehearsed speech was in vain, because after a couple of rings it went into voice mail, and there was no way I was leaving a message. I'm not very good at voice mail messages at the best of times. And this was so not the best of times.

I picked up my bag and car keys. I'd intended to go to the hospital to see Mr Lawrence anyway. If I caught up with Mrs Biscuit, she might know where Joe was, if he was still in the area. And, hopefully at the same time, I could persuade her to rethink her decision to leave Brackwith — although I wouldn't blame her if she refused.

At some time the previous night she'd told me Mr Lawrence had been taken to F ward on the second floor. So I hurried through the hospital reception area and followed the directions towards the ward. As I walked down the long corridor, I gave a sigh of relief as I saw her in the distance.

I hurried towards her. Two uniformed policemen were walking side by side, and I had to dodge past them to reach her. 'Mrs Biscuit,' I called, my voice echoing along the corridor. 'Ivy. Please wait.'

She turned towards me, her face deathly pale, her eyes wide. Was it bad news about Mr Lawrence? I stepped towards her, intending to put my arms around her and give her a big hug.

'Thank goodness I've caught you,' I blurted out before she could say anything. 'Is Mr Lawrence all right?'

She stepped away from me and nodded without speaking.

'Oh, thank goodness for that. Look, I just want to say how sorry I am for being such a complete moron, and to ask if you know where Joe — '

I stopped at the sight of the expression on her face. She looked shocked — I could almost say horrified

— to see me. How had things got so bad between us?

'Look, I really am so, so sorry . . . ' I began again, but stopped when I realised she wasn't looking at me at all, but over my shoulder. I turned to see that the two policemen I'd hurried past were now coming towards us, both wearing the same grim expression, both looking at her.

'Are you Mrs Ivy Biston?' the taller of the two asked. 'We've been trying to trace you. We'd like you to come with us, please.'

'What's this all about?' I demanded, but they ignored me.

'We think you may be able to help us with our enquiries into the attempted murder of William Edward Lawrence,' the other one said.

'But that's ridiculous.' I said as the tall one took the basket from Mrs Biscuit's hands and looked inside. 'What was in here?' he asked sharply.

'The — the pies I cooked yesterday,' she said.

'And what have you done with them?' His eyes narrowed as he moved closer to her. 'Did you give them to Mr Lawrence? Is that what you're doing here?'

'No, of course I didn't. I gave them to the girl on reception,' Mrs Biscuit said, her voice low and frightened.

He nodded and turned to his colleague, his voice urgent. 'You take her down to the car,' he said as he hurried away. 'I'll go into the ward and check it out.'

'But where are you taking her?' I called after them. 'Can you at least tell me that?'

'The police station,' he said as he took her by the arm and led her away.

'Don't worry,' I called to Mrs Biscuit as I ran down the corridor behind them, 'I'll follow you. You'll need a lift once they realise they've made a huge mistake.'

But as I jumped into my car, I saw the clock on the dashboard. How could it be lunchtime already? Luke was due out of school in just over half an hour.

Once again, I dialled Joe's number. But this time I let it ring, cursing as it went through to his voicemail. No choice now but to leave a message and hope he was still in the area. 'Hi, Joe. It's Beth. Look, I'm sorry about ringing you when you could be on your way back to London. If you are, then please ignore this. It's just . . . I don't know . . . I suppose you can't . . . Sorry, I'm rubbish at leaving messages. It's just . . . I've got a bit of a problem and may be late picking Luke up from school, and he finishes at lunchtime today, being Friday. I don't suppose . . . No, chances are you're miles away. Forget it. It'll be fine. I'll sort something this end. Sorry to have troubled you.'

I drummed my fingers on the steering wheel. What to do now? That would teach me not to avoid the other mums at the school gates. I didn't know any of them well enough to have their phone number. Not even Fiona Farringdon-Smythe's. Especially not hers.

Then I thought of Simon. 'If there's anything I can do, just call me,' he'd said often enough. So I took him at his word and did just that. To my utter relief, he answered the phone almost immediately.

'Simon. Thank goodness I've caught you,' I said. 'I need to ask you the most enormous favour. I wouldn't ask if it wasn't important, but to be honest, I don't have anyone else to turn to.'

'It's OK, Beth,' he said soothingly. 'Just calm down and tell me what the problem is.'

'It's . . . ' I checked myself in time. The last thing I wanted to do was let him know that Mrs Biscuit had been arrested. 'I've been held up. In — in Kendal, and there's no way I'm going to make it back in time to pick Luke up from school. They finish at one-fifteen on a Friday, you see.'

'And you want me to pick him up?' He sounded surprised, and I thought for one awful moment he was going to say no. But then he said: 'Yes, of course

228

I will. At one-fifteen, did you say?'

'Yes. Is that going to be a problem?'

'Not at all. So where do you want me to take him? To Brackwith?'

I thought quickly. 'No, Mrs Biscuit's not there. She's — she went to the hospital this morning to see Mr Lawrence and is not sure what time she'll be back.' I was pleased at having explained her absence without telling the whole truth or an outright lie. Simon didn't need to know she'd been taken to the police station. I'd never hear the last of it. 'Can you take him to your office and I'll pick him up from there? Will that be a problem?'

'Not at all,' he assured me. 'I'd do anything for you, Beth. You know that.'

'Thanks, Simon. You're a star. I'll be as quick as I can, I promise,' I said. Much relieved, I drove off in the direction of the police station.

25

Simon put the phone down, leaned back in his chair and smiled. 'Well, what do you know?' he murmured. 'That couldn't have worked out better if I'd planned it.'

His secretary looked up from the adjacent desk. 'Sorry, Mr Chance, did you say something?'

'No, just talking to myself.' He closed down his computer and glanced at his watch. 'Look, I've got Mr and Mrs Wilson coming in at one o'clock. Can you ring them and put them off?'

'But it's ten to one now,' she said. 'They'll be here any minute. I think — '

'I don't pay you to think, Mrs Parker,' he snapped, a flash of colour high on his pale cheeks. 'Just put them off. Apologise for my absence. Say I'll ring them tomorrow. I don't care what you do — just deal with it, OK? I've got to go out.'

She frowned and reached for the phone, the expression on her face suggesting she was far from happy. He pushed his chair back, squeezed past her and grabbed his coat. When he moved into his new offices, he vowed he'd have a room to himself and not have to share a poky little room where there was only just space for two desks and a printer.

'When will you be back?' she asked.

He shrugged. 'No idea. I could well be out all afternoon. It all depends how things pan out. And don't try and call me either, because my phone will be off.'

'But what about — ' she began.

'Sorry, can't stop. I'm late as it is. Whatever it is, I'm sure you'll deal with it.'

He ignored her tut of disapproval and hurried out, promising that one of the first things he'd do when he got back was ring the employment agency and see about getting a replacement secretary. He'd inherited Mrs Parker when he bought the business last year. She'd been with old Mr Peterson forever, and Simon had found her knowledge of the business invaluable at the beginning. But she'd taught him all he needed to know, and it was time for a change. Besides, he'd need someone a bit more upmarket and attractive when he moved; someone who'd fit in better with his new corporate image, especially now that all his other plans were falling so nicely into place. Joe Tennant was safely on his way back to London, and Beth's ghastly cook was on her way too and would soon be out of the picture. And now, just when he thought things couldn't get any better, Beth had phoned to ask if he would mind picking up Luke from school. How brilliant was that?

He hurried to the car. As he looked back, he saw an elderly couple — Mr and Mrs Wilson, no doubt — approaching the office. They'd probably be so annoyed at his no-show that they'd go to another agent. But they were only after a little two-bedroom bungalow, so they'd be no great loss. He was never going to get rich on the back of the Wilsons of this world.

Beth Tennant, on the other hand . . . He found himself humming as a tune wound its way through his head. Yes; in the words of the song, everything was indeed going his way. It was indeed a beautiful morning. And it was only going to get better.

26

Having sorted Luke out, I turned my attention to Mrs Biscuit. I couldn't get the picture of her stricken face, as those policemen led her away, out of my mind.

I drove as fast as I could, but was held up by every set of traffic lights that seemed to be permanently stuck on red; every little old lady who couldn't decide whether or not she wanted to cross on every pedestrian crossing; every delivery wagon parked on every set of double yellow lines between the hospital and the police station. To say it was a long, frustrating journey across town was like saying Mount Everest is a bit on the big side.

But my frustration didn't end there, because when I eventually pulled into the police station there was nowhere to park, and loads of notices promising dire consequences if I parked in the wrong place. So I then wasted yet more precious minutes driving around the town, trying to find a parking space. I ended up parking in the town's main car park and sprinting back to the police station.

But my frantic rush was all in vain. When I arrived, dishevelled and panting for breath, there was no sign of her. She certainly wasn't hanging around outside waiting for me, as I'd imagined. I'd been so sure that when they got there, they'd realise they'd made a terrible mistake and let her go. Unless, of course, they'd already done so and she'd got a taxi.

But when I asked, the harassed-looking man behind the desk told me she was still there and advised me not to stay. She was in the interview room, he said, and there was no telling how long she'd be there.

'Is there anything I can do?' I asked. 'Do I need to get her a solicitor or anything like that?'

He shook his head. 'She'll be advised of her rights where legal representation is concerned, ma'am,' he said, then turned away to answer his phone.

I checked my watch. I didn't want to leave her there, but what could I do? Luke would be out of school by now, but I didn't want him hanging around the police station with me while we waited for Mrs Biscuit. On the other hand, I didn't want to impose on Simon's good nature any longer than I had to. Luke could be pretty hyper when he came out of school, particularly on a Friday, and I wasn't sure Simon would be able to cope with his nonstop chatter. And if Luke started on about 'rashers of wind' or any of Mrs Biscuit's other choice descriptions, I could just imagine the look on Simon's face.

No, best to collect Luke as soon as possible. I'd decide what to do about Mrs Biscuit later. So I drove back to Ambleside. Simon's office was in a little side road just off the main street, which was packed with parked cars and pedestrians. Not a parking space in sight. I left the car in the main car park and hurried off to collect Luke.

A chill wind tugged at my coat as I took a short cut through the park. It sent the last of the fallen leaves whirling around on the path ahead of me. As I stopped to do up my coat tighter, I looked up and saw in front of me the two rows of trees Mrs Biscuit must have been talking about. They were drab, spindly things at this time of year, but I was pretty sure they were indeed the ones that in the spring were festooned with long golden chains that formed a spectacular archway across the tarmac path. Today, of course, there were no leaves on them, but several shriveled-up seed pods still clung like forlorn little flags to some of the otherwise bare branches.

So these were the seeds that, according to Mrs Biscuit, may well have been the cause of Mr Lawrence's collapse. Out of curiosity, I reached up and picked one of the pods and slit open the dry, crackly casing with my fingernail. Inside lay the little black seeds. So small and innocuous-looking. Hard to believe they could cause such problems. I put them in my pocket, then began to walk the short distance to Simon's office.

Seeds . . . The park . . . Had I been really, really stupid? I stopped so abruptly that a woman with a buggy almost cannoned into me. She swerved to avoid me, giving me a full-on glare as she did so.

Simon was always picking up seeds and putting them in his pockets; I used to tease him about it. And he walked through this park to his office every day. And he'd been alone in the kitchen, with Mrs Biscuit's half-finished pie still on the table.

But no, he couldn't have. He wouldn't have. It was ridiculous of me to even think it of him. He had no reason to do such a terrible thing. He was my friend. And yet, he had been very angry with Mrs Biscuit that day. More angry that I'd ever seen him. Even so . . .

I shouted a hasty apology to the young mum whose buggy I had nearly derailed and began to run, praying that I was wrong. Please, please, please, let me be wrong.

27

Joe left the stuffy, overheated office where he'd been for the last hour and a quarter and took a grateful lungful of cold, fresh air. It had been a long, tedious wait, but worth it to confirm his suspicions. When Joe had eventually got to see him, the man from the Environmental Health Office had been understandably cautious and anxious about breaches of confidentiality. Yet as Joe explained the circumstances, he unbent a little, and said he was keen to help.

'I can't comment on a particular case, Mr Tennant. I hope you understand that,' he said, looking down with a frown at the notes he'd been making while Joe was speaking. 'But let me assure you, no one from this office would have made that phone call. We would certainly not take it upon ourselves to phone a business's individual customers in the manner you've described. We simply don't have the manpower — and even if we did, we wouldn't take that sort of action. It would be wholly inappropriate. I'll question my staff, of course; but once again I can assure you that the phone call you've just described didn't come from this office. And I'd be very interested to discover where, in fact, it did come from. We always take malicious calls of this nature very seriously indeed.'

Joe nodded. It was exactly as he'd thought. He'd had plenty of dealings with Environmental Health officers over the years, most of them amicable and professional. When Beth had told him that morning that one of her customers had had a phone call purporting to come from the EHO advising her to cancel a planned stay because of an outbreak of food poisoning, the whole thing had struck a false note. So he'd requested an interview with the local office; and, although it had taken a long, boring wait to see someone, it had been so worth it.

But if it wasn't the Environmental Health Office phoning Beth's customer, then who? Who would want to damage Beth's business in that way, and why? The whole thing was making him very uneasy, and if he hadn't already decided to stick around for a couple more days until he was sure that there would be no more nasty surprises for Beth, then this would have changed his mind. Not that she'd thank him for it, though. He'd made such a bad move that morning, offering her the money. What was it about Beth that always made him say the wrong thing to her? He was usually so good at reading people, but with Beth he got it wrong every single time.

And that was before he even thought about telling her about him and Andrew — that last bitter row.

And now she was thinking of selling

Brackwith after all. He should be relieved. After all, it was what he'd wanted for her; what he'd come up here to advise her to do. But he knew the depth of feeling she had for the place. So what had happened to make her change her mind? Maybe he should go back to Brackwith later this afternoon, tell her about the visit to the EHO, and try to sound her out about her plans.

And who was she planning to sell to? The more he learned about Simon Chance, the less he liked him. For starters, he was pretty sure he hadn't been a friend of Andrew's as he'd claimed. Joe had known all of Andrew's friends and Simon wasn't one of them. So why would he pretend he was? Was it to get close to Beth? No wonder Ivy had been so worried about him hanging around that she'd contacted Joe and asked him to come up here and check Simon out for himself.

Well, he'd made a few enquiries, and the more he learnt about the guy the less he liked him. According to one of his old climbing buddies he'd had a coffee with this morning, Simon had seriously overextended himself to buy out old Mr Peterson's estate agency, and business was pretty thin on the ground.

She wasn't going to like it, but he was going to have to sit Beth down and share his concerns with her. She'd probably rip his head off, but he'd deal with that.

But first things first — he needed to call the hotel and extend his booking by a few days. And then, of course, there was Kate. He took out his phone, intending to ring his PA and ask her to send her some flowers, with his apologies. When he got back to London he was going to have to go around and see her, apologise properly and break things off with her, assuming she hadn't already broken things off with him. She was much too nice a woman to be messed around with in this way.

He had turned his phone off, as it had buzzed just as he was going into the meeting with the man from Environmental Health. As he switched it back on, he saw that he had three missed calls, one of which was from Beth. When she'd walked away from him at Brackwith this morning, he'd got the impression that she never wanted to see him again. So what was she calling about?

He listened to the voice message but it didn't make a lot of sense. Beth wasn't kidding when she said she was rubbish at leaving messages. That was about the only bit of the garbled message he could understand.

28

As I raced across the park, a whole series of pictures clicked through my mind, like a slide show when the mechanism's gone ballistic. Simon's office just minutes away from here. His daily walk from the car park through the park, under the laburnum arches. Stopping to pick something up. Then came pictures of Simon alone in the kitchen at Brackwith while I went to answer the door to Joe. Mrs Biscuit's half-made pies on the table. Simon, biting back the anger when he overheard Mrs Biscuit's less than complimentary description of him. Then, minutes later, his barely suppressed fury when I turned down his client's offer.

Of all the pea-brained idiots. How could I have been so stupid? So naive? So blind? It could only have been Simon. He had to be the one who put the seeds in the pie. And now — panic gripped my throat — now he had Luke.

Without stopping to look, I ran across the busy road and earned a blast of a horn and a volley of curses from a white van man for my pains. 'Tired of living, lady?' he yelled.

For the second time in as many minutes, I shouted out an apology and kept on running, running, running. I arrived out of breath and panicky at Simon's office. No Simon. No Luke.

'Where is he?' I yelled as I burst through the door.

His secretary — a grey, beaky-nosed woman — looked up like a startled heron. 'It's Mrs Tennant, isn't it? Are you all right? You look quite pale, my dear. Would you like some water?'

I shook my head. 'Where's Simon? And Luke?'

'Now you're not to worry,' she said with a smile. 'Mr Chance rang just a moment ago with a message for you. He said to tell you he's got Luke and that he'll see you at Brackwith.'

'At Brackwith?' My heart gave a

lurch. 'But he was supposed to bring him here.'

'Here?' She looked surprised. 'But those were his exact words. He made me repeat them, like I'm some sixteen-year-old not used to taking messages. 'I've got Luke,' he said. 'When Mrs Tennant arrives, tell her that, and that I'll see her at Brackwith.' As for meeting him here, I think there's been some sort of misunderstanding between the two of you. When he left here, just before one, he was quite adamant he wasn't going to be back this afternoon. Made me cancel his afternoon appointments and left me to deal with a very unhappy couple of clients, I can assure you. I told him — '

I didn't wait to hear any more but ran back to the car park. As I ran, I called Simon's mobile. No answer. When I reached the car, I tried again, and again it went straight to voicemail.

'Simon,' I gabbled, beyond caring about what sort of message I was leaving or whether or not it made any

248

sense, 'I don't know what sort of sick game you're playing or why. And I don't care. Do you understand? I don't care. All I care about is Luke. Don't hurt him, please. He's only a little boy. Your quarrel, whatever it is, is not with him. I'll do anything, sign anything, whatever. And I promise I won't tell the police it was you who poisoned Mr Lawrence. Just don't hurt Luke. Please, Simon. Please.'

I hardly remember the drive back to Brackwith. If there were any little old ladies dithering about on pedestrian crossings this time, or delivery men parked on double yellows, I drove unseeingly past them all. The only thing I could think of was getting to Brackwith. And Luke.

When I pulled into the yard, Simon's car was already there. I hardly gave myself time to turn off the engine before I leapt out and raced across the yard, calling Luke's name.

'Luke, Luke, where are you?'

But there was no answer. Only

mocking echoes of my own voice that bounced back at me off the old stone walls.

Then Simon appeared from the narrow space between the two barns. He was alone. 'How did you know?' he asked. No friendly smile this time. His eyes, beneath those sandy eyelashes that Mrs Biscuit was so right to be wary of, were like flint.

I ignored his question and ran towards the nearest barn. 'Where's Luke? Is he in there? What have you done with him?'

'He's quite safe.' He stood between me and the door. 'And he'll stay that way as long as you do what I say. And you can start by answering my question. I'll ask you again — and this time you will answer me. Got it?'

I nodded.

'You said in the message you left on my phone that you knew it was me who poisoned Mr Lawrence. How?'

I forced myself to stay calm for Luke's sake. I turned and looked towards Simon's car, but there was no sign of him there. So he had to be in one of the barns. But which one? If I chose the wrong one, Simon would be there before I could reach him.

'How did I know? Well, you're a keen gardener, and there are laburnum trees near your office, in that lovely park where Luke likes to go skateboarding.' I inched forward as I spoke, trying to get closer to the barn. Hoping, too, that Luke would hear my voice and not be too frightened. 'You're always picking up seeds, aren't you? You probably had some in your pocket, like I have in mine at this very moment, when you came here yesterday. I picked some up on the way to your office, and that's when I realised. I left you alone in the kitchen where Mrs Biscuit had been making the pies while I went to answer the door. So it could only have been you.'

'And have you told anyone this theory of yours?' he asked.

I shook my head. 'And I won't, I promise, if you'll just let Luke go.'

'Of course I'll let him go. Just as soon as you do what I ask.'

'Which I will. Whatever it is,' I said quickly. 'But what I don't understand is — why, Simon? What had poor Mr Lawrence ever done to you? He's an asthmatic and it made him horribly unwell, you know.'

'The old man didn't do anything. But that cook of yours is a rude, thoroughly unpleasant woman,' he said, an angry spot of colour staining his pale cheeks. 'I'd just found out about the poisoning scandal at that school she used to work at, and was on my way to tell you about my client's amazing offer for this place, when what should I find on my way across the park but laburnum seeds? It seemed like fate, particularly when I got up here and found she was in the middle of making pies. Then, when you left me alone in the kitchen, it was all I could do not to burst out laughing. Talk about falling into my lap. I figured if you or one of your guests became ill, a quick phone call to the police and she would be implicated, which of course she was. You should've listened to me when I tried to warn you about her, Beth. I was doing you a favour.'

'A favour?' I was only a couple of feet away from him now, inching ever closer to the barn. 'How do you work that out?'

'Before she came along, your business was going belly-up, and I'd been softening you up nicely to sell the place. You should've taken the offer I made yesterday, you know.' He gave a thin, cold smile. 'The price has dropped now, of course.'

'I don't care about the money,' I said quickly.

He shrugged. 'Just as well, then. Still, it's a pity about the old man, though.'

'A pity? You could've killed him.' I choked back the words 'you idiot'. 'It was touch and go for a bit.'

'He was a casualty of war, I'm afraid. This poisoning thing was a touch of genius on my part. I figured that not only would it implicate your cook, but your guests would be queuing up to cancel. And I was right, wasn't I?'

'No,' I lied, refusing to give him the satisfaction of knowing his callous plan had worked. 'People have been very understanding.'

'Including Mrs Turner?' he said with a cold smile. 'That's not what I heard.'

'How did you — ?'

'You know, in these days of identity theft, you really should be more careful about leaving names and contact numbers around. The Turners' details were among all that unsightly clutter on the dresser in your kitchen for anyone to see. No wonder you can never find anything. And they were ever so grateful to me for the warning. Unlike you.' He glared at me. 'You shouldn't have upset me yesterday by turning my client's offer down without even pretending to think about it. It was a very good offer.'

'Is that what this is about?' I was within arm's length of him now, and I longed to swing my fist and hit him. Very hard. 'You'd poison a man and kidnap a child, just to sell a house?'

'There's more at stake here than this wreck of a place,' he said. 'If you must know, I overextended myself financially when I bought old Edward Peterson out. The bank was worse than useless and refused to help, so I was forced to take up some dodgy loans. I now owe some seriously nasty people a seriously nasty amount of money, and they've agreed to take payment in kind. Run-down properties like this ripe for development at knock-down prices — otherwise, they say, I'll be the one getting knocked down. Permanently, if you get my drift.'

'But even so — '

'Enough talking.' He put his hand in his pocket and drew out a piece of paper. 'I can't hang about. Let's go indoors and get this signed, shall we?'

'Not without Luke,' I said as I backed away from his outstretched hand. 'You can't seriously think — '

'For heaven's sake, woman!' His voice rose shrill, his eyes wild. He looked and sounded like a man on the edge; like he'd been holding himself in check but had now suddenly lost it. 'What the hell are you waiting for? The longer this takes, the worse it is for the kid. I don't make empty threats, haven't you worked that out yet? Shall I tell you what will happen to your precious little boy if you don't sign?'

'No, please,' I cried. 'Give me the paper. I'll sign it. I don't care about the house. You can have it. Just let Luke go. Please.'

But as I put my hand out to take it, I heard the sound of a car pulling up behind me. Then came the best sound in the world.

'Mummy?' Luke called out, his voice filled with indignation. 'You forgot it was Friday again, didn't you?'

29

'Luke?' I whirled round to see him getting out of Joe's car. What was going on? My head was spinning as I tried to take it in. He wasn't with Simon at all? But Simon said . . . He let me think . . . I rounded on him as the fury that bubbled up inside me threatened to boil over.

'You — you — ' I began, but got no further. Simon rushed at me, his eyes wild, his narrow face contorted with rage. Before I realised what he was going to do, his fist crashed into my shoulder and I staggered back, falling heavily as I did so. I cried out in pain as my arm scraped against the rough stonework of the barn wall as I went down.

'Are you all right?' Joe asked as he ran across to help me to my feet while Simon zigzagged away across the yard, heading for the gap between the two barns. 'What happened?'

'I'm fine,' I gasped, reeling as much from the shock of the attack as the actual blow. 'It's Simon. Don't let him get away. He — '

But before I could explain, a long drawn-out scream rang out. Simon windmilled through the air, matchstick arms and legs flailing, before he hit the hard concrete of the yard with a sickening crunch. Luke's skateboard, which he was usually very good about putting away, lay upside down, its wheels still spinning. Simon lay moaning in a crumpled heap beside it. I'd tell Luke off about leaving it lying around later. For now I was deeply thankful that he had.

'Are you all right, Mummy?' Luke peered at me anxiously. 'You've got blood all down your arm and it's dripping on your jeans.'

'I'm fine,' I assured him, searching in my pocket for a tissue. 'I just scraped my arm on the barn wall, that's all.

Come here and give me a big hug. That'll make it better.'

I held him close and made a silent vow that I would never, ever let him out of my sight again. Year Two trips to Coniston, rugby matches, dates with girlfriends, whatever. For the next fifteen years at the very least, I'd be there beside him, like a limpet on superglue. Helicopter parents would have nothing on me.

I looked across the top of Luke's head at Joe, who was now kneeling beside Simon. 'Is he OK?' I asked.

'It looks like he's broken his leg,' Joe said as he took out his phone. 'I'll call for an ambulance. Then let's get him into the house. Do you think you can stand if I help you?' he asked Simon.

'No,' I said sharply. 'He's not coming in to the house.'

Joe looked up at me, puzzled. 'Beth? We can't leave him out here. He's hurt.'

'I'm sorry, Joe.' I glared down at Simon. 'He's not coming into the house. He can go in the barn. It's warm and dry. He can stay there until the ambulance comes.'

If it was up to me, Simon Chance could stay out in the yard and freeze to death. And for two pins I'd happily break his other leg, plus an arm or two, for what he'd put me through. And for even thinking about harming my son. I held Luke closer, but he wriggled out of my grasp and retreated to a safe distance in case I tried to hug him again.

I opened the barn door while Joe helped Simon up and half-carried him into the barn. He sat him in an old garden chair just inside the door. Simon leaned back in it, his face grey, his eyes squeezed tight shut against the pain.

Joe phoned for an ambulance then turned to me. 'Look, am I missing something here?' he asked quietly. 'What's going on between you and Simon? And what have you done to your arm? How did you come to fall over?'

'If you'll stop firing questions at me

long enough, I'll tell you,' I said with a pathetic attempt at a smile while I tried to get my chaotic thoughts into some sort of order. 'I didn't fall — he pushed me, and I've got the bruise on my shoulder to prove it.' I glared at Simon, who was slumped back in the chair, his eyes still closed. 'But that's the least of it. This — this lowlife told me he'd kidnapped Luke,' I went on in a low voice so that Luke wouldn't hear. Even though he was now halfway across the yard on his way to retrieve his skateboard, that boy had hearing as sharp as a bat's when it suited him.

'He told you what?' Joe's eyes darkened.

'It was when the police took Mrs Biscuit away,' I began. 'But you don't know, do you, Joe? They arrested the poor love at the hospital this morning. Said something about the attempted murder of Mr Lawrence, if you ever heard anything so crazy. But it wasn't her who poisoned the pie. It was Simon. He admitted it to me, just now.'

'Don't be ridiculous.' Simon's eyes shot open and he looked towards Joe. 'I said no such thing. She's being hysterical.'

'Is she, now?' Joe said. 'But it ties in with what I've found out. I've spent most of the morning hanging around the council's Environmental Health Department trying to discover who made the phone call to the Turners and why. They denied all knowledge of it. But it was you, wasn't it? You made that call. I thought maybe you were just taking advantage of what was simply a horrible accident by spreading a rumour to serve your own ends. But if you were the one who put the poison into the pie in the first place . . . '

'Of course it wasn't,' Simon blustered. 'Don't listen to a word she says. She always was a flakey one. First kidnapping, now poisoning. What is she going to accuse me of next? I ask myself. Well, I'm going to sue her for every penny she's got. Leaving things like that skateboard lying around for people to fall over . . . The place is nothing short of a death trap.'

'Be quiet,' Joe snapped, then turned back to me. 'And Luke, kidnapped? Was that what your message was all about? I have to say, Beth, it didn't make much sense.'

'I'm sorry. But when the police took Mrs Biscuit away, I was in a state of complete panic,' I said, ignoring Simon's snort of derision. 'I couldn't bear the thought of her going through all that on her own, so I told her not to worry, that I would be there. Only then I realised it was Friday, and Luke's year finishes school at lunchtime on Fridays. So I rang you.'

'I'm sorry; that must have been when I was in the council offices. My phone was turned off.'

'I just assumed you were on your way back to London. So I phoned Simon. He was always offering to help; and, fool that I was, I thought of him as a friend. How wrong can you be about someone?' I gave Simon another glare.

'Anyway, I asked him to pick Luke up from school and said I'd collect him from his office in town as soon as I could. But I didn't know then he was a complete lunatic, not to mention a criminal. I think we should call the police.'

'And tell them what?' Simon said. 'I didn't kidnap him, did I? How could I, when all the time he was with his uncle? Now do you see what I mean about her being flakey?'

'You let me believe you'd taken him,' I said, and turned to Joe. 'He left a message with his secretary to say he'd taken Luke to Brackwith. Then when I got here, he said Luke would be quite safe provided I signed some piece of paper he had with him. I imagine it was to do with selling Brackwith, as he's been on and on about it for ages.'

'I'm an estate agent,' Simon said. 'I was a merely acting on behalf of a client. It was a very generous offer.'

Joe turned on him. His voice was very controlled. 'I thought I told you to be quiet,' he said, but it was the look in his eyes that made Simon shrink back in his chair.

'The paper's probably still there in his pocket, if you don't believe me,' I said.

'Of course I believe you,' Joe said. The warmth in his eyes was nearly my undoing. I felt my anger begin to slip away, and with it my self-control. My throat constricted and two fat tears slid down my cheeks.

'He — he said that if I didn't sign, he'd . . . ' I couldn't go on. I closed my eyes and took a deep, steadying breath as I relived those nightmare moments.

'Miss Doble is very, very cross with you, Mummy,' Luke said as he came into the barn. 'She wouldn't let me go home with Simon because you hadn't filled in a form to say he could collect me. I might've stayed in school on my own all night if Uncle Joe didn't come.'

'I don't think it would have come to that,' I said. But my heart sank at the realisation that once again I was in Miss

Doble's bad books.

'Anyway, there was no harm done,' Joe said as he turned his attention to the graze on my arm. 'Look, I've got a first-aid kit in my car. Or, of course, this might be the moment to give that flashy first-aid kit you've been boasting about an outing. Where is it?'

'I know, Uncle Joe,' Luke said. 'I'll get it, shall I?'

'OK,' I said. 'And get the blanket from the chair by the Aga while you're there,' I called after him as he raced off into the house. Much as I hated Simon and what he'd tried to do to me, I didn't like the way he was starting to shiver. And his face had gone alarmingly pale.

'I don't really need first aid though,' I said to Joe, but nevertheless made no attempt to pull my arm away. His hand felt warm and comforting against my wrist. 'It's just a scratch, as you can see.'

'I told Miss Doble Joe was my uncle, didn't I, Uncle Joe?' Luke said when he returned in record time with the first-aid tin and the blanket, which Joe placed over Simon, who was now shivering violently.

'Indeed you did,' Joe said as he prised open the first-aid tin.

'I told her that he was my uncle even though he doesn't come to our house very often,' Luke went on, looking at Simon with undisguised curiosity. 'Has Simon eaten too many plums, like Mr Lawrence did?'

'No,' I said. 'He fell on your skateboard, which is why I'm always telling you not to leave it lying around. And he's hurt his leg very, very badly.'

Luke obviously decided it was time to steer the conversation away from skateboards left lying where they shouldn't and back to Miss Doble. 'And then she said I could go with Joe even though you hadn't filled in a form for him, Mummy. Because Miss Doble said she knew Joe so that was all right. Mummy, I'm starving. Can I have a biscuit?'

'OK, go and get one,' I said, then turned to Joe, my eyebrow raised. 'You and Miss Doble — ?'

'We go back a long way,' he muttered as he gave what I can only describe as a slightly sheepish grin before he bent his head to examine the cut on my arm more closely.

I never thought I'd be grateful to Miss Doble and her endless forms, but I was. Because if Simon had been allowed to take Luke, who knew how it would have ended. Nevertheless, I felt a flicker of . . . well, I don't really know what it was, to be honest. Only that something inside me gave a little flicker of discomfort at the thought of Joe and the colour-coordinated Miss Doble going back a long way, whatever that meant.

I gave a sharp intake of breath as Joe put some antiseptic cream on the cut, then expertly bandaged it up, his large, capable fingers incredibly gentle.

'I'm sorry,' he murmured. He fastened off the bandage, but his hand still rested on my arm. 'Did I hurt you?'

I shook my head. Somehow I'd lost the power of speech as I looked up into his eyes. Why had I ever thought them grey and cold? They were warm and kind; concerned. But there was something else there as well. Was I imagining it? My throat felt suddenly dry and I ran my tongue across my lips.

Joe, too, seemed as affected by the moment as I was. We both took a step towards each other, as if drawn together by an invisible thread.

'Well, that's one way of getting your hands on the place, Tennant. I'd heard you were a win-at-all-costs merchant when it came to getting what you want, but that takes the biscuit. Maybe I should have tried it on with her.'

We jumped apart, startled by Simon's harsh voice. For a moment I'd forgotten all about him. Forgotten about almost everything. I even forgot to breathe. Now as my breathing restarted, my heart began to pound like a jackhammer. 'Joe, don't listen to him,' I begged. 'He's just trying to wind you up.'

I stopped as I saw the expression on Joe's face. The years rolled back, and it was like we were facing each other across Andrew's open grave again. The same cold look. The same barely contained anger. He was looking at me like he hated me.

My stomach heaved, and for a moment I thought I was going to be sick. I pulled away from him, turned and hurried towards my car. 'Luke?' I called. 'Come on, quickly. We're going into Kendal to collect Mrs Biscuit. She should be ready to come home now.'

'Can Uncle Joe come too?' Luke asked as he skipped along behind me.

'No,' I said quickly. 'He's got to wait here for the ambulance to arrive.'

'Can I wait with him?' he asked.

'Definitely not,' I said, remembering my vow not to let Luke out of my sight for the next fifteen years.

'Beth?' I paused for a moment as I heard Joe call after me. 'I'll be here when you get back. We have things to sort out. We need to talk.'

Now why, I wondered as I started up the car, did that sound like a threat?

30

Ivy checked her watch and was surprised to see it was almost three o'clock. She'd been in the police station for the best part of three hours, and it was beginning to look like she'd be there for another three, when one of them had just that moment come in and told her she could go. Just like that. No explanations. No apologies. Just, 'You're free to go.'

'Do you need to see me again?' she asked as she stood up.

The older one, the one who'd played the good cop during their good cop/bad cop routine (Ivy watched all the TV detective series, so she knew how it worked), smiled kindly at her and said, 'Probably not. I'm sorry we kept you so long, but in a case like this we have no choice but to act on information received. But I've finally managed to get hold of the headmistress of the school, and she's confirmed your version of events concerning the accidental poisoning of one of the pupils, and that you were in no way implicated in that.'

Ivy swallowed hard. So the headmistress had come through for her after all, bless her. At one stage Ivy was beginning to have her doubts, especially when it was all taking so long.

'So, your information received — where did that come from?' she asked.

'I'm not at liberty to tell you that.'

'You mean it was an anonymous call, do you? Was it a man?'

'I'm sorry.' He shook his head. 'I can't tell you that either.'

Ivy frowned. Who could it be? Who hated her enough to make all this trouble for her? It simply didn't make sense. Except, of course, if that man was Simon. But even then, why would he go to all that trouble?

'Mrs Biston?' The policeman opened the door. 'I said you're free to go. You can stay here if you like, but there's someone waiting for you in reception.'

She followed him along a bewildering maze of dreary corridors decorated with unrelenting posters full of dire warnings about drugs, drop-outs and drunk drivers. She was touched when she reached reception and saw that the person waiting for her was Beth. She was bent over her phone but jumped up at the sight of Ivy, her face lit up by a big beaming smile.

'Beth, lovey, you haven't been waiting here all this time, have you?' Ivy asked anxiously. 'Only, there was no need.'

Beth shook her head. 'No. In fact, you won't believe what's happened since you've been in here. For a start, I now know who put the poison in Mr Lawrence's pies — and if they'd only listened to me in the first place — ' She looked pointedly at the man behind the desk, who turned away and focused on the screen in front of him. ' — they'd have figured it out too.'

Ivy was unable to resist saying, 'It was Simon, wasn't it?'

Beth's eyes widened with surprise. 'Yes it was. But how did you know?'

'Because I've been sitting here for nearly three hours with nothing better to do than trying to puzzle it out. I knew it wasn't me, or you, or Joe. And according to the lab report, it was definitely laburnum seeds. They actually found some in the remains of the pie I brought in. And obviously they'd been introduced deliberately. So that only left one possibility — it had to be Simon. He was the only other one there. But why he would do it; what he had against poor John — I mean, Mr Lawrence — I don't know.'

'Let's talk about it in the car, shall we?' Beth said, linking her arm in Ivy's and steering her towards the door. 'I'll bet you can't wait to get out of here.'

'You don't know how much.' Ivy lifted her face to the sky as they stepped outside. The dreary November day, cold, grey and overcast, suddenly seemed as light and bright as a spring morning after the overheated windowless room she'd been sitting in for the last three hours. 'Do you mind dropping me at the hospital, lovey?' she asked as they reached Beth's car. 'Only, I left my car there.'

'Of course.'

'Now, you were saying what Simon had against John?' Ivy asked once they were in the car and Beth was threading her way through the town's busy traffic. 'I didn't even know he knew him.'

'I'm afraid he did it to get at me,' Beth said. 'Poor Mr Lawrence was a 'casualty of war'. That was how Simon so charmingly put it.'

'He told you that?' Ivy said. 'What did he mean?'

'He didn't care who ate the seeds, just as long as someone did. Then the talk would be that we had a problem at Brackwith, with guests getting poisoned, stuff like that. The sort of story that could easily put me out of business if it got around. Which, of course, he made jolly sure it did. He was the one who phoned the Turners, pretending to be from the Environmental Health Department and advising them to cancel their booking.'

'He was probably the one who phoned the police and told them about the incident at the school as well,' Ivy said. 'But I don't get it. Why would he go to all that trouble?'

'He wanted the business to fail so that I'd be forced to sell Brackwith at a knock-down price to one of his crooked mates he owed money to. He said . . . It was horrible; I was so frightened. I — I thought . . . ' Beth's voice faltered, and her knuckles whitened as she tightened her hands on the steering wheel.

'Oh lovey, don't upset yourself, particularly while you're driving. Tell me later.'

'No, I'm fine, honest. If anything, I'm angry now, more than anything. Besides, we're here,' she went on as she drove into the hospital car park. 'Where did you leave the car?'

Ivy showed her, then waited until she'd pulled up alongside her car before asking, 'So what did he do?'

'He let me believe he'd kidnapped Luke to force me to sign an agreement to sell,' Beth said. 'Though really, he hadn't. Joe had picked Luke up from school. But I didn't know that. I was ready to sign. Much as I love Brackwith, I love Luke a whole heap more. But before I could sign, Joe and Luke turned up. Joe had got my message and collected Luke from school instead of Simon.'

Ivy drew a sharp breath. She'd always disliked Simon, with his thinning, slicked-back hair, his simpering smile and sandy eyelashes. What she would give for five minutes alone with him. Just five minutes. 'The monster. He let you believe he'd kidnapped Luke? Have you told the police?'

'Of course. I gave them my statement while I was waiting for you, and they're on their way to the hospital to interview him right now.'

'The hospital?'

Ivy felt a glow of satisfaction as Beth

went on to explain about the accident with Luke's skateboard and Joe's opinion that Simon had probably broken his leg.

'Pity it wasn't his blooming' neck,' Ivy commented. 'And Joe — where is he now?'

A shadow chased across Beth's face. 'He — he stayed with Simon to wait for the ambulance,' she said then went on quickly, 'As for Luke, you'll never believe this, but I was just parking the car when we bumped into the dreaded Fiona Farringdon-Smythe. It turns out that her Josh and Luke are best mates, and Fiona asked if Luke would like to go back to their house as Josh has a new signal box he's dying to show off. I didn't even know the boys liked each other, least of all the best friends bit, but what do I know? Anyway, it worked out perfectly for me, because I really didn't want him hanging about the police station while I gave my statement. Not that I told Fiona anything about that, of course. And I offered to come by and pick Luke up later, but she said she's happy to give him tea and bring him home herself. Do you know, she's actually quite nice when you get her away from that little gang of hers.'

Ivy had the feeling that Beth was talking nine to the dozen to stop her asking any more questions about Joe. But she didn't push it.

'Ivy?' Beth said as Ivy went to get out of the car, her voice hesitant, her forehead creased in a worried frown. 'You — you are coming back to Brackwith, aren't you? I mean, you're not still cross with me over what I said this morning?'

'No, of course I'm not, lovey.' Ivy patted Beth's hand, anxious to reassure her. 'And I will come back. You try and keep me away. But first I'm going to pop in and see John. I thought I'd let him know the latest developments. I doubt the police will bother to keep him informed.'

'John, is it now?' Beth murmured with a smile as Ivy got out of the car.

'Yes, I'm sure he'll want to know.'

'He asked me to call him John, that's all.' Ivy felt her face growing hot. 'There's no need to make a big thing about it, young lady.'

Beth laughed. It was so good to hear her sounding a bit more like her old self that Ivy didn't even mind that she was the cause of her amusement.

'My dear Mrs Biscuit, I'm not the one making a big thing about it. Or going the colour of a beetroot,' she pointed out, still laughing.

'I'll be off now and leave you to your nonsense,' Ivy said, reaching for the door handle. But then her face became serious and she turned back to face Beth. 'There's something else I want to ask you, pet. John told me this morning that the hospital have said they'll discharge him, most likely tomorrow, provided he has somewhere to go where he'll be taken care of. Now of course, I'm not expecting you to do that, but if you — '

Before she could get any further,

Beth threw an arm around her shoulders and hugged her tight. 'You shouldn't even have to ask,' she said, her voice husky. 'He can stay as long as he likes. And as a friend, not a paying guest.'

'You're a good girl,' Ivy said. 'I just wish you and Joe — '

Beth pulled away. 'Best not keep John waiting any longer,' she said. 'Tell him I'm looking forward to seeing him back at Brackwith.'

Ivy sighed as she watched her drive away. Joe and Beth. What was it with those two? It was a crying shame. Two such lovely people; they were so right for each other, but they just couldn't see it. But it wasn't her place to interfere, much as she'd love to.

Her heart gave a little skip as she went back over the conversation she and John had had that morning. It was the one thing that had kept her going through that long, scary time in the police station. 'Ivy, my dear,' he'd said, 'you have brought nothing but joy into my life and that's the truth.'

Then it had been clouded by the spectre of the poisoning hanging over her. Now that was all over, however, and her stomach was once again doing the dance of a thousand butterflies.

All over? Who was she kidding? There was the small matter of telling John about the incident at the school and how she should have prevented it but didn't. She'd been about to tell him that morning when the rottweiler of a ward sister had come bursting in and shooed her away like an errant sheep. This time, though, she would stand her ground.

If her and John's relationship was going anywhere, then there were to be no more secrets. She'd tell him the truth and leave it up to him to take it further. Or not. Although, of course, she very much hoped he would.

31

The ambulance picked its way gingerly down the rough track from Brackwith, its bright yellow bodywork a vivid slash of colour against the high grey stone walls that banked either side of the road. Joe watched it disappear with a deep sense of relief. If he'd had to stay there with Simon for a minute longer, he'd have broken his other bloody leg.

When he thought what that little rat had put Beth through, it was all he could do to keep his hands off him. He'd made better use of the time, though, and put a bit of distance between himself and Simon at the same time by contacting the police while he'd waited for the ambulance. He'd told them about his visit to the Environmental Health Department that morning and convinced them that they really needed to interview Simon about the poisoning, as he had means, motive and opportunity and had boasted to Beth about having done so; and about the malicious call to the Turners. They were very interested and assured him that they were en route to the hospital to question him right away. Simon Chance was going to have some company to while away the hours in A&E.

Joe kicked at a loose stone, sending it scudding across the yard. What sort of monster would do that to a young mother? But then, he thought with a rush of guilt, who was he to talk, taking advantage of Beth by coming on to her when she was at her most vulnerable? Wasn't that what he'd been about to do back there? No wonder she'd scuttled away from him like a frightened rabbit.

What would have happened, he wondered, if Simon hadn't spoken out when he did, and called him a win-at-all-costs merchant? Did Beth really believe that what he wanted from her was Brackwith?

He checked his watch and settled

down to wait for however long it took for her to come back. This time he would not back away, but would tell her the truth — the real reason he and Andrew had quarrelled so violently that last day. The thing that had haunted him all these years.

Andrew had been in a foul mood ever since they'd set off that day. Not only that, but he was reckless; simmering. Joe had seen that mood before and knew the signs. It was Andrew getting ready to bail out. Obviously he'd had enough domestic bliss, and the news of Beth's pregnancy would have been the final straw.

Joe should have kept his opinions to himself. But when Andrew had started spouting on about how Beth had tricked him, first into marriage and then into parenthood, he hadn't been able to contain his anger and had told his younger brother a few home truths. Starting with the fact that he needed to grow up and face his responsibilities for once in his life.

'Or what?' Andrew squared up to him in a way he'd never done before. 'What are you going to do if I walk away? Step into my shoes? Isn't that what you've always wanted? Don't you dare criticise me, you bloody hypocrite. You've had the hots for Beth ever since I first introduced you. Don't think I haven't noticed. You're not very good at hiding your feelings, bro, at least not from me. It's written all over your face every time you look at her.'

'Don't be ridiculous, Andrew,' Joe said. 'I'm going down now. We'll talk about this later when you've calmed down.'

Joe began to walk away, but Andrew shouted after him. 'You can bloody well have her,' he said. 'I'm out of there.'

It was the way he said it, like Beth was a piece of merchandise he'd grown tired of. Joe whirled round, eyes blazing, first clenched. He took a step towards Andrew, his fists raised. Would he have hit him? He'd never know, because Andrew stepped back, away from his raised fists.

It was a step too far.

For the rest of his life, Joe would never lose that last image of his brother: the shock on his face when he realised he was falling. This time there was nothing Joe could do to help him.

Of course, he'd never tell Beth what Andrew had said about her. That would be too cruel, and chances were he didn't mean it anyway. Andrew always did have a reckless way of speaking when he was wound up. Beth was obviously still in love with him, and Joe didn't want to do anything to tarnish his memory. And she needed to know the part Joe had played in his death. Maybe then he'd be able to find some peace. Because the thing that tormented Joe most of all and made him, even now after all this time, still unable to look her in the eye was that Andrew was telling nothing but the truth.

Joe had been in love with Beth since way before Andrew had died. She was the reason he could never make a relationship with any other woman work. Her face haunted his dreams. She was the only woman he would ever love.

He was responsible for his brother's death, and he was in love with his widow. What sort of monster did that make him?

32

As I turned into the yard at Brackwith, my heart sank when I saw that Joe's sleek silver car was still there. I was hoping that once the ambulance had left, he would have gone too; that he'd changed his mind about that 'little talk' he'd decided we were going to have.

He was sitting in his car but got out as I pulled up. 'You're still here then?' I said, and regretted it the second I saw his eyebrows lift.

'You were, no doubt, hoping I'd have given up and gone away,' he said, and his voice was back to that clipped disapproving tone I knew so well. 'I'm sorry to disappoint you. I said we needed to talk, and that is exactly what we're going to do.'

'Look, Joe, I've had a long, stressful day,' I said, trying to keep the pleading tone out of my voice. 'Can't this wait?'

'I'm sorry. It can't.'

He didn't look very sorry to me. I sighed and headed for the house. 'You'd better come in, then. I'll put the kettle on.'

'I don't want a cup of bloody tea!' he snapped. 'I just want you to stay in one place long enough to hear what I have to say.'

I turned round. Obviously whatever he had to say to me wasn't going to take that long, which was a relief. Probably yet another lecture on how I was throwing good money after bad and that I should cut my losses and sell Brackwith. A chill wind blew across the yard, and I shivered as I braced myself for the inevitable.

First, though, I wanted to get my bit in before I lost my nerve yet again. I owed him that much. 'Joe,' I said quickly, 'about this afternoon . . . I don't know how to begin to thank you for what you did. If you hadn't been there — '

'Well, I was,' he said. 'I'll always be

there for you, Beth. You should know that by now.'

'I'm beginning to. It was you who settled my overdraft yesterday, wasn't it?' I said. 'Why didn't you tell me?'

'Who did tell you?'

'Mrs Biscuit, of course. We had a bit of an up-and-downer this morning, and she said it was about time I learnt a few home truths. That you'd been covering my back for years. She made me feel ashamed of the way I treated you. That's why I was trying to get hold of you earlier today, to say sorry and to thank you for bailing me out. And, of course, to say that I'll pay you back as soon as possible.'

'You have nothing to apologise or thank me for,' he said. 'And I'm sorry if at times my desire to help has come across as interfering or controlling. I know how much you value your independence. And I admire you for it.'

'But?'

'But what?' His eyebrows creased in a puzzled frown.

292

'There's a 'but' coming, I can feel it. So go on, say it. Let's get it over with, then I can go inside and get warm. I'm freezing to death out here.'

'Do you need a coat? I've got one in my car.'

'No.' My voice came out sharper than I'd intended. I didn't want another fight with him. I was tired of fighting. 'Joe, for heaven's sake, just get on with it. You're going to give me another lecture on how I should sell this place and move somewhere more sensible, aren't you?'

'What?' He stared at me like he thought I was losing my mind. Which, given the strain I'd been under for the last few days, was probably not far from the truth. 'Beth, I've not come here to talk about Brackwith, but about Andrew. About the day he died.'

I froze. Just when I thought the day couldn't get any worse, it did. Well, I'd vowed I wasn't going to put it off again, so I took a deep breath and went for it. 'You're right, of course. We should talk about it. And I know what you're going to say,' I said quickly before I lost my nerve. 'You blame me, don't you? And — and you're right to do so, Joe. Because it was my fault he died. I'd pushed him too far, you see. He'd never been as keen on the 'settling down and setting up home thing' as I was. Then when I told him I was pregnant, it was the final straw. We had this blazing row, and both said things we shouldn't have. He said I'd trapped him into marriage and now was trapping him into parenthood. He ended up by saying you'd been right about me all along; that I was a spoilt, selfish brat who — '

'I never said that. Well, perhaps at the beginning, before I got to know you properly, when I thought you were just playing at house. But when I saw how hard you worked and how good you were for Andrew — '

'Not good enough, obviously. He accused me of having deliberately got pregnant and told me he was leaving me.'

Joe went to speak, but I was in full flow and would not be stopped until I'd said what I should have said a long time ago. 'Tying Andrew down was like trying to cage a wild bird. I'm so very sorry, Joe.'

He didn't answer; just stared at me, a stunned expression on his face. This was worse, far worse, than anything I had imagined. He looked like I'd just dealt him a body blow.

I reached out and took his hand. It was ice cold. 'It's taken me a long time to get my head around this, but I now realise Andrew wasn't ready for marriage, least of all parenthood. But I pushed him into both. He was right about that, although he was wrong about my having got pregnant deliberately. That was a total accident. But I figured I wanted it badly enough for both of us so it'd be OK. Only it wasn't, was it? I knew how reckless he could be when he was angry, but I still escalated the row just before he went climbing. Maybe I thought that would stop him going, but I also knew that Andrew dealt with confrontation by walking away. Which was, of course, exactly what he did. By the time I'd calmed down, I tried to phone him, but it was too late; his phone was out of range. I cost you your brother, Joe. Can you ever forgive me?'

He put his hand over mine. 'You — you think I blamed you?' he said, his voice husky. 'All these years you've thought that?'

I nodded. 'That day at the funeral, you looked at me as if you hated me.'

'You thought I hated you?' His eyes still held that stunned expression. 'That couldn't be further from the truth. Beth, I hated myself, not you. And when I've finished telling you, you will as well.'

He freed his hand from mine and stuck it deep into his pocket. Then he looked out across the valley and up towards Brackwith Fell, where a pair of buzzards drew lazy circles in the fading afternoon light. 'You weren't the only one to have a row with Andrew that day,' he said in a low monotone. 'And like you, I knew how reckless he could be when he was angry. And yet, I went on and on at him to tell me what was wrong when I should have stood back and let him sort things through for himself.'

'The row was about me, wasn't it? He told you he was leaving me.'

'I was so bloody angry with him, I — I went to hit him. And he — '

'You hit him?' I whispered when it became obvious he wasn't going to say any more.

He shook his head. 'Not exactly. I raised my fists at him but pulled back. I didn't hit him, but I might as well have done. He — he stepped back. It was icy. He slipped. And then he — he fell. One minute he was there; the next . . . I couldn't save him. I tried, but . . . '

He closed his eyes, but not before I'd seen the glint of tears in them. 'You apologised to me just now for costing me my brother,' he went on before I could say anything. 'But the truth is, I cost you a husband and Luke a father. I was the one who made him take that careless step backwards. I'm the one who should be apologising to you.'

'You didn't cost me my husband. The truth is, I'd already lost him. Our marriage was as good as finished.' My head cleared, and for the first time since that terrible moment the policeman had appeared on my doorstep, I realised the truth. And, as I did so, the guilt I'd carried on my shoulders for all that time rolled away like early-morning mist. Now it was time to do the same for Joe.

'Joe, you didn't make Andrew lose his footing that day any more than I did. It was an accident. A horrible, tragic accident. No one caused it to happen, or wished it to happen. No one was to blame, except maybe to an extent Andrew himself. He was the one who stormed off, who behaved with reckless disregard for his own safety — and, I don't doubt, yours as well. He knew the danger of the mountains as well as you did. He was a grown man, even if he didn't always act like one. And, do you know what? I don't blame you for his death. I never did. But I don't blame myself either. Not anymore.'

I pushed my fingers through my hair, straightened my shoulders and stood tall. It was like I'd just shrugged off this heavy grey blanket that had weighed me down for years. Did Joe feel like this as well? I sure hoped so.

'Oh, Joe.' I took a step towards him as tears of relief prickled my eyelids. 'Ivy would say we're a right daft pair — and she'd be right, wouldn't she? All these years I've been thinking you blamed me, and you've been think-ing — '

'No, Beth.' He stepped back, one hand outstretched, a warning not to come any closer. 'There's something else. Don't you want to know what Andrew said that made me want to lash out at him?'

'Is there any point? It was all such a

long time ago now.' The seriousness of his expression was beginning to worry me and I gave a little laugh, hoping to break the tension. 'In the words of that song that all the kids in Luke's school sing all the time, let it go.'

But he didn't laugh. He didn't let it go either. 'I can't,' he said. 'You need to know. He accused me of being in love with you, though he didn't put it in quite those words.'

My brother's got the hots for you, Andrew said one evening when we'd had a couple of beers too many. We both treated it as a joke, as far from the truth as it's possible to get. The 'man with a calculator for a brain' and the woman whom he described as a spoilt brat who 'screamed and schemed' to get what she wanted. Hardly likely, was it?

I tried for the lightly amused look, but that's not easy to achieve when your cheeks are red enough to stop traffic, and that hole in the ground — the one you're praying will swallow you up — never materialises. 'That was typical of Andrew, wasn't it?' I was quite proud of how cool I sounded. 'He never was any good at reading people. After all, you'd never made any secret of how you felt about me.'

'Oh yes, I did.' His eyes were fixed intently on mine. 'I did make a secret of how I felt about you. Andrew had got that right, at least. You see, Beth, I was in love with you.'

For once in my life I was clean out of words. Whatever I'd been expecting him to say, it wasn't this. Somewhere on the fellside, a sheep was bleating. Rooks were calling in the tall larch trees. A dog barked. But in the yard, there was silence — apart from the thudding of my heart.

'I've shocked and embarrassed you,' he said. 'I'm so sorry. I shouldn't have come. I won't bother you again.'

He turned and walked towards his car. But before he reached it, something inside me clicked. That spark that had always been between us ... I'd assumed it was because we hated each other. But what if . . . ? I remembered how good it had felt when he put his arms around me after Mr Lawrence was taken off to hospital. I'd felt safe; comforted. But it was more than that, wasn't it? I remembered, too, that moment in the barn when he'd bandaged my arm, the pull that I'd felt to move into his arms. What would have happened if Simon hadn't intervened?

'Joe, wait.' I couldn't let him go like that. As I walked towards him, he turned round, his face still troubled.

'I shouldn't have said anything,' he said. 'I'm not proud of the fact that I coveted my brother's wife. It's not sat easily with me all these years. Not that I'd have done anything about it, of course. And then after Andrew died, I made a vow that I never would. I hoped you'd find someone else and move on. I was shocked beyond belief when I saw you at his graveside that day, still obviously mourning him. The guilt was almost unbearable.'

'Was that why you never came to see us?' I asked. 'Until now, that is.'

He nodded. 'I came because Ivy asked me to. She was worried about Simon sniffing around — with good reason as it turned out.'

I shuddered at the memory. Later I'd thank her and Joe for being there for me and Luke when we needed them. For now though, it was important I got across to Joe the truth about my feelings for Andrew.

'I never regretted marrying your brother,' I said, choosing my words with care, 'even though our marriage was tempestuous at times, to say the least. But he gave me the best thing in my life, and that's Luke. And I'll always be grateful to him for that. But, Joe, I don't still mourn him. As I said, had he lived, we'd have been divorced years ago and I'd still have been a single mum.' I gave a small shrug as I smiled up at him. 'I'm embarrassed to tell you that the real reason I was in the graveyard was that I was early for school and didn't want to get caught by the playground mafia.'

He pushed his fingers through his hair and grinned back at me in a way that reminded me of Andrew, back in the early days of our relationship. Why did I ever think the two brothers were polar opposites?

'Having run the gamut of them myself this afternoon, I can well understand that,' he said as some of the tension in his face slipped away.

'I wish I'd known at the time how much you helped me over the years,' I said. 'First Sally, then Mrs Biscuit. And, of course, paying off my overdraft this week. Why didn't you tell me?'

'I guess I was afraid you'd think I was trying to buy your forgiveness; that you blamed me for the accident,' he said. 'Added to which, you made it pretty damn obvious you couldn't stand the sight of me. Any offer of help from me would've been met with a firm 'thanks but no thanks'. Isn't that so? You were always so icily polite.'

'Me, polite?' My voice shook and I could hardly breathe as I moved closer to him. I hoped — no, prayed — I wasn't just about to make the biggest fool of myself; that I hadn't completely misread the situation. 'That wasn't politeness. That was fear. You used to scare the life out of me.'

'And now?' he asked. His eyes bored into mine, like he was looking into my very soul.

Slightly more confident now, I placed my hand on his arm and pulled him gently towards me. 'Do I look like I'm scared?'

We were so close, I could smell the musky scent of his aftershave; feel his breath on my face and the tension in the muscles of his forearm where my hand rested. *I used to be in love with you*, he'd said. And now?

With a little murmur that was half-groan, half-sigh, he pulled me into his arms and touched my lips with his. Feather-soft. Infinitely gentle. He pulled slowly back, and I saw the answer to my question in his eyes.

'Joe?' I whispered. And then we came together in the sweetest, most tender kiss that turned my knees to water and left me wanting more.

'I've wanted to do that for so long,' he said, his voice shaky.

'Then what are you waiting for?' I asked.

His answer was another kiss. Deeper, more urgent. And definitely not very brotherly.

Above us, a buzzard, outstretched wings silhouetted against the falling light, wheeled away and vanished over the top of Brackwith Pike with effortless ease. He called and, seconds later, was followed by his mate.

Then I heard Andrew's voice. *Good on you, girl. Take care of him*, he whispered as he faded away.

We all had other mountains to climb now.